CREATIVE CHAOS

JORIA OLIVA

MICHAEL RAY KING   T. G. AGIN

ROBIN H. SOPRANO   MEL JOHNSON

MRK Publishing

PO Box 353431

Palm Coast, FL 32135-3431

www.MRKPublishing.com

Printed in the United States of America

Table of Contents

Introduction

The intent of Creative Chaos sprung out of an idea for a group of writers to challenge themselves and write something outside their norm. The group of five writers contains a mix of gender, genre, experience, and publication level.

Each writer submitted a story (or two) as well as information about themselves and even about the writing of their particular story. All hope that these samplings of their work will inspire you, the reader, to seek out their other writings.

Sit back, get comfortable, and enjoy writers not only challenging themselves, but enjoying the writing process as well…

Jorja DuPont Oliva

Alien Encounter

"You want to kiss me, don't you?" Jolene beams, dragging her finger along her tongue and plump bottom lip, adding a shimmering, moist glow. Resting her head in Justin's lap, she relaxes in the lush green field of wildflowers as the sun polishes each vibrant bloom. A slight breeze gently wisps her blonde curl in front of her thick lashes. She wipes the strand of hair from her face to gaze into Justin's eyes. "We are perfect together..."

"We are, Jolene." Justin grins, still admiring her gold skin with the tips of his fingers. He strokes the locks of blonde hair that have spilled over in his lap, flowing toward the terrain beneath where they lay.

"How can we be so perfect? Yet I can't help but believe…something still seems to be missing."

"Come on! Chase me!"

Jolene rolls from Justin's lap, giggling as she rises from the ground.

"Chase me!"

She sprints through the field of flowers, peeking over her shoulder, making sure Justin follows.

He finally arrives at her side; Jolene reaches for his hand and pulls him along through the field. They both wrap together and plummet into the bed of flowers. Justin rolls on top of Jolene and cups her sweet face in his hands. He pulls her mouth toward his as she whispers, "You want to kiss me…"

"You want to kiss me…" Jolene glitches.

"You want to kiss me…"

Remnants of Jolene's face ripple in Justin's cupped hands.

Lips clinging together, not wanting to detach. Lack of oxygen calls for an inhalation.

That would be my idea of an affiliation with her. With Jolene. The wish to stay fastened almost takes over my will to live and breathe. Jolene Carson feeds my biggest craving, my need. I relish my moments with her. Every vivid image that graces my eyes, my mind, and—if only—my lips. Her earthy essence. I love her more than life itself. Is it conceivable to love a human? A human who is only a part of my mind and has no physical form?

It is possible. I know I love Jolene and spend every moment I can with her, virtually. The only hope of being together rests in an earthly contraption. Jolene is the only woman I've ever known, with the exception of my mother, of whom I have a vague recollection. I suppose I loved my mother, but it was my need to have her nurture me that produced our bond. I lost my mother when I was small, and Justin is the Earth name I gave myself the year the Tri-voids attacked the planet Earth. My ship crashed while Tri-voids took over Earth. Our galaxies were at war over natural gas resources. Now I am here, stranded on Earth after my beings destroyed everything, took what they needed, and departed back to our planet—leaving me behind.

I assume it has been two years, according to the passing of this planet's days. I leisurely remove the virtual headpiece, the only reality that exists for me here on Earth. I feel earthly. Never was I comfortable in my Tri-void scales, and I have fallen in love with an Earth woman, Jolene. A virtual Earth woman. As far as I am concerned, I am more human-like than I ever was Tri-void. I feel things—not physically, but in my insides. Emotionally. In human terms, my amygdala has enlarged as a result of my virtual experience with human personalities and their feelings, a weakness my fellow Tri-voids consider earthlings to suffer from.

I reach down and stroke the top of the Earth creature's head. A trivial, furry mammal that licks, yaps, and is always anxious to have me as a companion. Another plus for planet Earth, Tri-voids consider any positive reinforcement unacceptable to our genetic makeup. A feebleness.

Human life forms on planet Earth appear atypical. Organisms flourish, and the possibility of human beings exists, but in the two years, I have not encountered any. Only mammals—including swine—

and some reptiles walk the desolate land in which I have taken up residence, and various birds fly through the once-busy sky.

Utilizing only the virtual headpiece to learn the earthly humans' way of life and means of survival was difficult, but I persevered. I have also learned to speak all of their languages, especially English, which is the language Jolene speaks.

A movement in the partially charred brush catches my attention. The Earth creature yaps its way to the vegetation and stops, anxiously wagging its tail, just at the edge. Crouched in the woodlands at the end of the desert sand, something shudders, wearing only stains of carbonized earth and nothing of material matter. The furry creature has found a human life form, and it appears to be of feminine composition. Could I possibly become fond of a physical human presence?

"#$&&)-@!%*(-?@:<>." I correct my language. "Hello, Earth being."

I reach down to this female being but notice my hand is a Tri-void hand. Pale green and only three long, thin fingers. Quite unlike how I have perceived myself when interacting with Jolene. Self-consciously I pull my hand back. The Earth being notices my insecurity with her. Tri-voids do not exhibit weakness or insecure behavior. I am adapting to my environmental stimuli.

"I will not harm you." I have also just employed compassion, another human trait.

The woman, too, appears to be unsure of interacting with me. The shivering of this being has given me a good indication she has fear of me, of my beings, the Tri-voids.

She finally speaks: "Please don't hurt me…"

"I mean you no harm. I have earthly food—berries, nuts…Here."

I push the earthly gathering toward the frail body hiding in the brush.

With its tail still wagging anxiously, the furry Earth creature sniffs this female being. This behavior is a good indication that the new female human is harmless, non-aggressive. The Earth female grabs the food, shoveling it in as quickly as she is humanly capable. This being seems to be starving. Unlike

Jolene, this being's skin is pale beneath the charred stains. Her hair is a dark brown, much like the furry creature's. The diversity among human life forms is astonishing. Each one is individualistic in nature, much like their languages. Unlike the Tri-voids, my beings. We all share a sameness that keeps our emotional capacity at a monotone state, possibly due to modified genetics that our imperials control in our DNA before conception. To strengthen our physical and intellectual makeup, to reduce feebleness, they say.

"What's your dog's name?" she asks as soon as she has consumed a fair amount of the gatherings, a sign she feels less frightened of my nature. She pets the furry creature's head. "He looks like a Yorkie mix."

"Dog's name?" I respond, realizing I had not learned as much about the human language as I had thought. Perplexed by the fact that they name their creatures as if they, too, were human. "He has not been named. I find he responds simply to the sight of my presence. He seems to show signs of joy. Even when darkness arrives, bringing a wide spectrum of stimuli, his emotional responses tend to stay mostly positive."

I crouch to the female's level to show I mean no harm. A mutual connection. Human-like.

"Spectrum. You should call him Spectrum." The female shows her teeth, rubbing the top of the creature's head as she calls him by the name, Spectrum. Odd, but the creature responds to the name and the touch of this human. This creature seems to enjoy wearing a name.

"Spectrum, a continuous range or series. Seems to fit," I respond as a human would. Conversation seems of great importance to human life. I suppose the virtual contraption taught me this.

"Why are you still here? I...I mean, didn't all your kind leave? You aren't coming back, are you? You got everything that Earth could offer you." She scoots backward into the brush. She looks as though she is frightened of me again. Her memory has brought the fear of my beings back into her vision. Recollection seems to be more profound in human beings. Tri-voids' ability for recall is adequate but less likely to cause emotional disturbance. I could hear her heart rate increase just as the thought of her memory surfaced. Emotion physically affects the human body.

"No, no. I am stranded here. This is my new home. I am not like them…" I try to explain my purpose in interacting with this being. "I promise I am no longer here to harm human life. I have become quite fond of Earth beings." I show her the virtual contraption. "I have learned you, your beings' ways."

She slowly emerges from the brush and solemnly asks, "What is your name?"

"Tri-voids have no names. We are very much all the same."

She starts to scoot into the brush again; I hold my hand up to stop her. "Justin. My Earth name is Justin."

She settles again, as if my having a name made me quainter. I reach my hands to her once more, and this time she latches on. My pale-green scales turn glittering in color. Many brilliant colors. Something I had never encountered. Her touch has changed the appearance of my scaled skin to a sparkling magnificence. We both watch, fascinated. Her heart rate decreases.

"You scintillate me...just from your touch." A touch I have so desperately desired to feel from my time with Jolene. Warm, soft, and gentle humanity. A craving, wish, yearning, and hunger filled my inside. Something non-Tri-void-like.

The furry Earth creature yaps as the female being's touch transforms my scales into a beige color of skin. The scaled texture of my outer coating had dissipated into soft, smooth, human skin. My three long fingers were now five with one pultruding from the side. I not only was adapting to my environment, I was mutating to become something that I have longed for. Human.

***

"He is returning to normal," a female's voice says. "His vitals have returned. His brain activity has started to rejuvenate."

Justin's eyes begin to flutter. Light surrounds him as people in white suits and coats pass into the room. They circle around the stainless-steel bed where he lies. He is confused. Had he only dreamed he was a Tri-void? What is happening to him? He looks down at his hand, which appears human. One of the workers in white coats hovers above his face. Justin notices wording embroidered on the right breast pocket of the white coat the female is wearing. The embroidery reads:

Tri-void Corporation

Could all of what he had known only been virtual? Was his life as a Tri-void only an experience? What about Jolene? Was she, too, an experience…within an experience?

"Justin? How do you feel?" the female in the white coat that seemed to be taking care of him asks. She strokes his sweat-soaked forehead and removes the electro-lines from his temples. "Justin, you did very good. You went further than anyone else in the study." The female looks familiar, almost identical to the female he had encountered on Earth, but her voice he recognizes as the virtual Jolene's.

"Is he realizing where he is? It can take a few minutes for his experience to dissolve," a male voice coaches from the right side of the room.

Another male voice jolts the female. "We did it. We have uncovered the human emotion link through analysis of original human DNA. We are going to change the world!"

She turns to Justin. "Justin, do you know who I am?" She cups his face. "It's me, Jolene…" Justin's lips pucker. "You want to kiss me, don't you?" She sharply turns her head, confirming with a life-size smile, "He's back…"

Jorja's Challenge

Although I've developed my own unique style as a writer, sometimes it's good to step outside of that space and speak with a slightly different voice. And for me, writing this piece in response to a writing challenge posed by our writers' group forced me to do that. However, some of my own voice and themes still come through. In this story, for example, my love of nature and Southern slang is still evident and metaphorical ideas are an integral part of the story.

I decided, then, to write this time within a specifically sci-fi genre and from an alien perspective. You guessed right, when I began to write the story I was like, "Who am I kidding?" I do not read sci-fi, and I am not even close to being a science buff. Therefore, for me, I REALLY challenged myself. Don't get me wrong, I love the *Star Wars* movies and all of the *Alien* movies, but they are movies. I had no clue how to begin writing a sci-fi tale. I have always admired the creativity displayed in that film genre, and I have wondered if particular films are based upon scientific evidence or just someone's crazy idea.

Getting back to my story, the metaphor I was attempting to get across within it is that no matter how much our leaders try to control us, what feels natural to us will always prevail and we will always remain who or what we were meant to be. I also wanted to show the power of the brain, how thought alone can affect us, just as my alien character is affected. This is part of the reason I used a virtual contraption as the tool for the alien.

I wanted to allow the reader to also see the beauty in our diversities as humans and to think about it from an unfamiliar admirer's point of view. In fact, my primary point was this: no matter how diverse we all are, there is always room for acceptance.

I hope I've conquered what I set out to do, and I hope you enjoy my short story challenge.

About the Author – Jorja

Jorja DuPont Oliva is the author of the Chasing Butterflies Series. With a hint of Southern charm, she weaves stories of magic into everyday life. She loves the imaginative elements as well as her characters' diversities in her stories. Jorja's debut novel—***Chasing Butterflies in the Magical Garden***—was published in 2013. By many readers' accounts, her stories are colorful, honest, and inspirational with a touch of innocence. Jorja's second book in the series—***Chasing Butterflies in the Mystical Forest***—was released in October 2014. Readers then continued on their magical journey with ***Chasing Butterflies in the Unseen Universe*** (October 2015), but this time with a more mature and evolved Dee and Lizzy, the series' enchanting main characters. Not only have her stories shown the growth of her characters, but also the growth of her writings.

Each story Jorja writes has a lesson to convey, as well. Her books employ symbolic meanings of nature's beautiful works of art, and her unique prologues also feature a view through the eyes of creatures of air and earth as they look at human struggles. The chapters contain quotes from all areas of beliefs and teachings, from Biblical, spiritual, and inspirational to self-help.

Never underestimate Jorja and her writings; she is always ready to brave new creative excursions. Coming up in 2017, she will be releasing her first psychological thriller—*SISTERLY*. Beyond that, you can never tell what voyage she will take you on next.

Excerpts from Jorja's books:

Mystical forest

"We are losing her!" Lizzy heard the voices fade down the hall. She walked out into the hall as Dee vanished from sight.

She crumbled to her knees. Joe came from around the corner holding flowers from Dee's garden in his hand. He dropped the flowers to the floor as he made his way to Lizzy.

"Lizzy?" he asked as he scooped her up.

"Joe, they were losing her... the baby...I can't lose her, Joe!" Lizzy babbled. Joe tucked Lizzy neatly into his strong arms and cradled her head.

Unseen Universe

"What is happening here?" I asked as we walked through the rainbow, into a field of sunflowers and daisies. Each flower pivoted towards the suns beautiful light, as if time was moving in fast forward, yet standing still at the same moment. "Sunflowers and daisy's together." I admired the sight.

"Sunflowers and daisies are part of the same family. They represent loyal love. The 'Asteraceae' is the largest flowering plant family and the name means, star." Dee smiled. "Star family," she added as she touched the giant sunflower cupping it in her hand.

"Absolutely beautiful." I admired the beautiful flowers.

Sisterly

"Hi, missy," echoed a high-pitched voice from a rocking chair by the front window as Janie entered the porch. There sat a petite elderly woman with hair as silver as chrome, her skin as pale as a powder puff as she held one of the calico cats in her lap. She looked like an old black-and-white photo cut out and repasted onto a color picture. I did not see her when I pulled in the driveway.

Books by Jorja DuPont Oliva

Robin H. Soprano

Gypsy's Gift

A memory, one that has been stuck in my head from about fifty-plus years ago, shoots around my mind. I look over at my eldest daughter sitting by my bedside, her eyes tired with puffy bags.

"Sarah," I whisper, still drowsy from another nap, "I have to tell you a story."

Her eyes search mine. "It's okay, Daddy. Tell me later when you're more awake."

"No, there is something I want you to know. I don't know how many more days or hours I have left on this earth, but rest assured, we are not alone. Don't be scared for me. I was given a gift, so to speak, I guess from heaven, or whatever powers that exist. I remembered this happened to my grandfather, too. Everyone thought he was hallucinating."

She looks at me deeper, eyebrow cocked in confusion.

"Daddy, what are you talking about?"

"Gypsy—where is Gypsy?" I ask.

"The dog? Daddy, what do you want the dog for?"

I take a deep breath. "Humor me; I'm old and I'm dying."

Sarah stands from her chair and hesitantly calls for my beloved dog Gypsy. The dog enters my bedroom with still a little pep in her old trot-like gait. My eyes meet hers, a little cloudy but still a nice whiskey-colored amber. Gypsy is a collie mix. Always loyal and smart, she's going on ten years old. She is healthy. I am not. Seems I basically have a rusty ticker. My heart is tired, and a cranky aneurism on a valve could blow any time. Luckily, I'm not in pain and don't need any medication except the pills that keep my blood thin. I'm just so darn tired all the time.

"Okay, Daddy, what is this talk about a gift?"

I summon the dog to get up on the bed as I prop myself up on some pillows. She complies and settles down, facing me. I motion to Sarah to sit back down.

She does with a sigh. Gypsy and I glance at Sarah then back at each other, and there it is: a voice. A beautiful voice like an angel in my head, but it's coming from Gypsy.

"She's not going to believe you."

"Before I explain this extraordinary thing, I'm going to tell you about Grandpa Marty."

Sarah curls up on the recliner next to my bed and throws a soft blanket over her legs.

Gypsy lifts her head, and her eyes meet mine again.

"Keep it brief. We all know you tend to ramble."

"I DON'T RAMBLE," I say firmly to Gypsy.

"I didn't say you did, Daddy."

I smile up at my daughter. "Sorry, sweetie. Wasn't talking to you."

Her face looks confused and a little frightened. "What…"

"It's what I'm trying to tell you. Look, just listen and keep an open mind, please," I beg.

"All right, Daddy. Go ahead."

"When I was about fifteen or sixteen, my Grandpa Marty's cancer had spread and he was in pain. His dog,

Muzzy, would sit on the bed day and night. We all thought, *Yes, Muzzy knows and he's watching*. Gramps every now and then would try to speak, and most of the time he didn't make sense. He was on heavy-duty narcotics, and he would babble much ado about nothing. He started to tell me and Grandma that Muzzy was talking to him. We kind of giggled but humored him. We knew it was the cancer and/or the meds.

"Back then, there was no hospice care, but Grandma got a nurse to come from time to time to help her when she needed or when my parents or other relatives could not be there. Nurse Basia. She was such a nice lady. She was already an old woman herself, and she was so caring and full of wisdom. She came here from Greece. She was so good with Gramps. He would do his babble thing, and Basia would answer him. One day I asked her, 'How do you know what he's saying?'

"She said, 'You must listen with only your heart. Your grandpa is in the middle of two dimensions right now. His human side is strong and wants to stay here on earth. His soul, however, is tired and wants to go home; it's pulling him to the other side.'

"Well, that blew my mind, as you could imagine. I told Basia, 'He thinks Muzzy is talking to him.' I laughed, but she gave me a look of such gravity, I froze in my sneakers. Then Basia glanced at Muzzy sitting there on grandpa's bed.

" 'Muzzy is talking to him,' she answered me with pursed lips. 'Most animals, especially dogs and cats, have a heightened sense of things. One must never assume they don't know what is going on. I believe Muzzy is communicating with your grandfather—not with a voice, but with his essence or soul. Animals are God's gifts. If we listen close, we can understand everything they tell us. Just because we don't see it or hear it, we can't believe it?'

"Daddy, are you trying to tell me you think Gypsy is talking to you?!" Sarah abruptly cuts into my story.

"Let me finish! Quit barking at me, would ya?"

Gypsy lifts her head again. *"She gets that from you, and she isn't barking; trust me."*

I give Gypsy a look and continue, "One night, I sat with Gramps. He was doing well on this particular evening, a little more coherent than normal. He told me some stories about when he was a boy and how he became a man. Things that made him proud and things that didn't. You know Great-Grandpa was a marine, had a bunch of medals? You know where all that stuff is, don't ya? Put it aside for that grandson of mine."

"Rambling…" Gypsy growls.

"I'm getting to it. This is *my* story, ya know."

"Okay, okay, Martin. Just get on with it, human. Look at her face. I'm sensing fear coming off her."

I observe my daughter sitting so still, not looking directly at me but through me. Fist under her chin, eyes a bit glassy. Gypsy is right.

"Sarah, please don't be scared. You need to trust me."

"Okay, Daddy, I'm listening. Yes, Joey will get those medals."

I take a deep breath. "Well, Great-Gramps told me Muzzy was talking to him, telling him it's a gift that our beloved animals share when they are given the chance to help them transition. I had forgotten about this until very recently. Gypsy came in here about five days ago, and out of the blue I heard her thoughts."

Sarah looks just a bit confused. "Transition? Daddy?"

I roll my eyes. "I'm gonna die Sarah. Gypsy has told me she can communicate with me at my final days to keep me calm and help me not to be afraid."

"Oh, my God, Daddy! Please! I think you're having a stroke!"

"I told you to keep it to yourself. There's that free-will clause again..."

"Sweetie, how can I make you understand...?" Then, an idea hits me. I look at Gypsy. "Give me something to make her see. Help me out here," I plead.

In response, Gypsy proceeds to tell me a little story, and I repeat it word for word.

"Gypsy says this is something only you and she would know. It was right before Joey was born. Hell, now I'm pretty sure it was about nine months before. Your mother and I went on that Alaska cruise, and you were coming by to take care of Gypsy, remember? So, one night you came over alone and you threw up in the kitchen sink. After you pulled yourself together, you ran out to get a pregnancy test. You came back here and took the test; it was positive."

Sarah cocks a nervous smile. "Okay, but everyone basically knows that."

"Yes, we do, but what we didn't know is what you said to Gypsy while waiting for the test results. You were sitting on the bathroom floor, Gypsy by your side, and you were crying. You told Gypsy, 'I hope if I'm pregnant this one goes full term.' Because you'd found out Mike had a chromosome deficiency that was making you miscarry, you went out one night, found someone to have a one-night stand with, and the rest is history."

Sarah leaps from her chair, shaking, turning white.

Gypsy stands up and barks at her. *"Oh, I think she's gonna pass out!"*

"Daddy, I...I...How did you find this out? I...I...don't understand!" she stutters.

"It's all right, sweetie. I'm not mad. I think you could have handled it a better way, but I get it. I'm not angry with you at all."

Sarah takes a few steps back and grabs her water bottle and takes a long pull from it, almost finishing it. After a deep breath, she speaks. "This isn't happening. Daddy, tell me you just knew all along."

I just gaze at my daughter, realizing at the time, the whole world must have been caving in on her.

"Daddy, I'm sorry. It was the only solution, Mike doesn't know Joey's not biologically his, and neither does Joey, and I want to keep it that way."

"Your secret is safe with me, but why didn't you come to me if there was no other solution? I would have helped."

Sarah cries harder. I can tell she's reliving it. "I…we…didn't have the money to go to a fertility clinic. I felt Mike slipping into depression, fearing he knew he was the problem and he wouldn't be able to give me a child. When the one test we did do showed it was not gonna happen with him, well, maybe I went a little out of my mind. This seemed to be the best idea at the time, and luckily it was." She chuckles through a veil of tears.

"Okay…shhhh, Sarah. Calm down, sweetie. Tell me, do you know the real dad at all?"

Her eyes go to the floor as she shakes her head *no*.

"Don't be embarrassed, sweetheart. It's okay, but what if you didn't get pregnant? Were you just gonna keep having one-night stands till you did?"

She throws her hands in the air. "I really didn't think about it, Daddy; please, can we drop it now?!"

"Okay," I whisper. "But this could have gone in a bad direction. Let's just say you were blessed."

Sarah looks at me, her face a tad serene. Gypsy just wags her tail then hides her nose in her paws. "Gypsy says 'Sorry,' but it was the only way to make you see I am in communication with her. So now do you believe us?"

Two big tears well up in Sarah's eyes. "Yes, yes. I don't know how or why, but yes, I believe you."

I observe my daughter as she composes herself, probably trying to wrap her mind around this bizarre yet magical fact. I glance at Gypsy.

"Do I want to know anything else about my other kids while we're on the subject?"

"That would be a no. *Some things are just irrelevant for you to know."*

"Hmmm…good. I can die happy."

"Ignorance is bliss."

"Daddy, why is Gypsy talking to you? Why now?"

"She says it's a gift that is bestowed upon certain animals and their masters. Some humans are sensitive to it, so I guess I'm like my grandfather. I suppose at some point you might want to tell your siblings about this. It may happen to one of you some day. Not sure if it's just the males. Gypsy has no answers to some of these questions—only that it helps us transition into the afterlife."

Sarah's eyes go wide. "So then there definitely is one, a...an afterlife? Heaven? Or a...another dimension?"

"I suppose so. I am not afraid now. This miracle she has given to me, it's like I can see for the first time or hear, just like Nurse Basia told me, with my heart."

I cough. I can't breathe; I'm choking. I feel as though I'm drowning. Congestive heart failure is coming on now. Sarah gets up to hand me a tissue, and Gypsy comes closer to my face and sniffs.

"Your time is closer, Marty. Relax; we are all here. I can show you a vision now."

I sit back in bed. I almost feel light or like I'm half way out of my body, and there right in front of me is my Adele, my wife of over forty years. She beckons to me, and she's smiling. I want to reach out for her, but Gypsy pulls me back in. *"Not yet, lover boy, but in due time. She is waiting, and she will be there to take you as soon as you go."*

Soon, the vision fades and I am staring into Gypsy's amber eyes again.

"Daddy, Daddy…Dad? Hey—you there?"

"Huh? Oh yeah, sweetie Gypsy gave me a…vision. I just saw your mother. She is waiting for me when I go. It's going to be soon, Sarah, very soon." My daughter smiles, her eyes glassy and moist. She is my strongest child.

***

The evening comes again, and I hear my children. All have grown into exceptional adults. They must have cooked. I can hear them having dinner, but I lost my appetite weeks ago. One by one, every few hours, they come in to check on me. I've developed a rattle in my chest now, and even I know it's called the death rattle. Gypsy is right: I'm not long for this world.

Sarah enters my room. "Dad, can you hear me?" I nod with my eyes still closed and hear the patter of paws and then feel my bed gently rock. I open my eyes as Sarah walks over and smiles. She kisses my forehead. "You have my secret, and I'll keep yours until I need to share. We are all here, Daddy, if you need us." She quietly leaves my room, and Gypsy and I are alone again.

"Marty, time is close. I can smell it. Are you feeling okay?"

I nod.

"I really can't explain how this is happening, but all you need to know is you should trust when I tell you we are not alone. I believe humans interpret heaven in many ways. You will understand more when you're there. You will receive an increased level of clarity, and you may remember being there once before. Yours

is a perfect human soul to my animal soul. On one occasion as a young pup, I remember how you scooped me up into your arms and I felt safe as I stared into your eyes and you stared back. My soul connected with yours and bonded with it as if I were a human baby. Then I did the same with Adele and the kids. I now had an exceptional pack. My instincts were to protect each of you, and I recognized you as the Alpha. And what an Alpha you were. I have devoted my loyalties to you."

I reach over slowly and scratch at Gypsy's furry chest. She raises her nose up and stretches her skin where I scratch. "Good ol' Gypsy. You are a good dog. Somehow I always knew what you needed."

"That was the connection I have felt since I was a pup. As I matured, you could understand me without speaking. I didn't understand your words then, either, but read your body language. I can sense when one of you has a bad day. I know when you feel sadness or joy. I knew, long before any of you noticed, when Adele was confused by the illness that deteriorated her mind. I can sense when any in my pack are ill, from the smallest of ailments to big ones. The day you had your

heart attack, I had sensed it coming for days, so I'd stayed close to you."

"Yes, I remember. You wouldn't even let me leave the house without you! My God, I couldn't understand why you were being so stubborn that week. You knew, huh?!"

"I knew some kind of bad thing was coming; when exactly, I couldn't be sure. I knew it was going to be life threatening. And when it finally came on, I tried to get you to hear me but you didn't. I knew you would come home again and we would have more time. But now we are at the end of the journey. It's just a matter of time, hours, now.

"Tell me, Gypsy…you showed me Adele. Is everyone I know there? Will I get questions answered?"

Gypsy stands on all four paws, stretches with her rump in the air, then pads in a circle, repositions herself, puts her pretty head on my knee, and lets out a groan. "What's wrong, girl? Don't you have an answer for me?"

She lifts her head again, eyes on mine. *"Adele will be there. Certain other people will be there, important ones in your life, individuals you have made an impact on and maybe some you might not have been kind to. Not all our loved ones may be present over there. They have journeys of their own. I can't say for sure who, what, or why, because everyone's path on earth is different. What I can tell you is this: the purpose of my gift is to calm you so you're not afraid to cross."*

I open my mouth to ask one more question and Gypsy cuts me off. *"No, I don't know anything about alien life or Area 51 or who killed Marilyn Monroe, so don't ask. And I don't know if you will find out once you are there. This is about you, Marty, your journey."*

I laugh. I laugh hard. I haven't laughed this hard in months. It hurts, and I start to cough and choke. Gypsy sits up to give me room until it all subsides.

"Well, how did you know I was going to ask that?"

"I know you, Marty. I know you like the back of my paw. Relax, my human. Your transition is near."

I sigh. "I wish I had more time. That is the only thing that pisses me off. Why do I have to go so soon and leave you all behind? I feel like I have so much more life to live."

"Almost everyone has that request. We never know all the answers, but remember, when you cross over, embrace the enlightened clarity."

The night goes on. I feel more and more like I am drowning, like my body is just shutting itself down. Gypsy snuggles by my side, and my children sit around in the room. I hear them chatting, but I can't join in. They are reminiscing about things like holidays or remembering things they did with Mom, too, and good times with Gypsy.

I hear, "Look, Dad's smiling. Do you think he can hear us?"

And I hear Sarah's answer: "Dad can hear more than you think; trust me."

I start to feel light. It feels as though my soul has disconnected and is just trapped inside a shell. My heart is skipping beats. I hear Gypsy say, *"Let go, Marty. Relax and release from your body. You can be free now."*

At first it's so hard to let go, but then I see a light and within it, Adele. She's calling to me. I want to go. I glance around to see Gypsy. She barks, and Adele grabs my hand.

***

"Daddy's gone," I say to my younger brother and sister. "He is at rest now." My siblings begin to cry a little.

My brother, Johnny, points to Dad. "He has a little smile on his face." We gaze at Dad and smile, too.

My sister, Samantha, the youngest of us, hugs me tight and whispers, "I hope Mommy was there waiting on him."

I turn my head to them both. "Yes, I believe Mom and Gypsy were calling to him."

"Gypsy?" My brother questions me. "You think Gypsy came for dad, too?"

I nod. "She was always by his side, so she came for him. She made Dad calm and reassured him that it's all right, just like he did for her and Mom when they couldn't go on anymore."

"Oh, I hope that's true. Do you really believe that, Sarah?" my sister asks.

"Yes, I do. Trust me…I do."

The end.

About my Story & Notes.

What if at the last moments of your life, your beloved pet gave you a gift. Though no words are spoken, you hear each other's souls. The effect it has on you is calming to help you cross over without fear or   doubt.

What if you were the only one who could hear them, see them? What if they showed you a life past and one waiting in the after, would you think you were hallucinating? Would your family believe you or would they humor you knowing your time is short.

I am part of a little local writers group in my home town. Every now and then we come up with ideas for fun. Part of this group is to keep us motivated in our writing and to help each other write through any blocks we have and, or write ourselves out of a corner.

On one particular day, I suggested I should write a short story, being I never had before and I hoped it jump start my passion for writing. One thing led to another and everyone decided to take the challenge.

We decided to write different from what we normally write about and take a step out of our comfort zone, after more discussions we decided to publish them in a compilation joint effort.

This was so much fun to challenge myself that I can't wait to write something else that is out of my norm. I usually write romance, and write from a woman's point of view. This time I wrote from a mans and a dog's. Still in keeping with a magical and or spiritual element I love.

I hope Gypsies gift touches your heart as it has touched my many beta reader's and friends!

About the Author – Robin

Robin H. Soprano born and raised in Essex county NJ moved to N. East Florida 25 years ago,

She found her love of writing and published two books. Magical /paranormal Romances, A Soul Mates Promise and Absinthe. Both can be found on Amazon and Barnes & Nobel web sites.

Her love for story telling grows strong and has no doubt she has big angels guiding her creative drive. She says she listens to gut instincts and her strong intuition. She is currently working on some other projects and hopes to get a few more books published. She spends her days enjoying a new life and path she was given. Also, loves reading and watching favorite shows and movies all in the company of her beloved dogs, Corey & Roscoe who make her smile even in her worst days. She currently lives with her boyfriend Harry, who she credits with giving her strength and encouragement in life as well as writing and reads what she's working on. She has a collection of Angels on a shelf in her office she looks to them every day and each has a special word to which helps her do almost anything….

DREAM ~ WISH ~ BELIEVE

Excerpts from Robin's books

A Soul Mate's Promise

I open my eyes and see Sal's handsome, smiling face.

"What's going on? What time is it?"

"It's about five. Sun won't be up for hours, but you were mumbling in your sleep."

"I was? What was I saying?"

Still exploring my body with kisses, his voice is muffled. "If I knew, I would tell you."

"And when I mumble in my sleep you wake me with kisses?"

"Yes," he continues between kisses. "You were starting to panic, and I wanted to wake you up calmly. Is it working?"

"Mm-hmmm."

"Good."

Sal rolls me onto my back and keeps me secure. He kisses my throat, then my breasts…

Absinthe

Without warning, men came. Marcellis Dubied had hired them to seek me out. First, they asked nicely for the remaining ingredient for my special elixir. Both Bernard and I told them that M. Dubied has the whole recipe. There is nothing more to tell. Dubied's men informed me that my sister, Jonet, had gone mad and leapt from a high window to her death.

I didn't believe them, of course. I know they must have killed her…

Three Blind Wives

We start to maneuver around and read men's profiles. Some were funny. Some were very dirty. And then there were a few normal ones.

Crystal was the first to go and text one of them. She keyed, HEY THERE WANT TO CHAT? Soon we all chimed in and found profiles of men that we thought would be fun to chat with and maybe set up a date. We synchronized up the website with our emails so when someone would respond we would know.

About three days in we were flooded with responses. As usual Crystal was the first to chat. His name was Brad. She set up a date on a Thursday night. She told us where and that she would text us if she was in any trouble. If any emergency occurred, we would swoop in for a rescue. The next night we would meet at Dusty's ranch for a girl's night and she would tell us about the date.

Books by Robin H. Soprano

Michael Ray King

Conflict of Interest

I am engaged to Marilyn, but Cindi is in my bedroom. She is on my bed. She sits there in jeans and a long sleeve white blouse, the top three buttons unfettered. She is all blue eyes and silky straight blond hair that falls just past her shoulders like pristine platinum icicles. The follicles must surely smell of strawberries or some exotic fruit.

Why am I doing this? I have a girlfriend. We've been together nearly four years. I've only known Cindi for three months. I know, I know. The first time I laid eyes on Cindi I began to fantasize about her. She is just one of those women you look at and think, "I wonder what she would be like naked?"

Is that crass? I'm sure it is. But is that an honest assessment of the situation? I'm sure it is as well. But why? What makes me shove Marilyn out of my mind and focus solely on this gorgeous woman in front of me? There must be something wrong with me.

I have never cared for men who did this kind of thing. Indiscretion so lacks honor and steadfastness and all those things I want to be associated with. My father was a dirty dog who slept around on my mother. Heck, in the last years of their marriage he openly cavorted with women, even bringing them to our house for private social engagements, if you catch my drift.

None of them were particularly attractive. I always thought that was odd. My father had the silver tongue and could swoon a woman visibly with his quick wit and disarming smile. So, was the fact that Cindi is runway-model pretty a step up from him? That just doesn't wash with me.

I know I shouldn't be doing this. Cindi is here because she had a fight with her husband. I should be consoling her instead of planning to bed her. She just comes across as a woman that wants to get laid. Often.

Sounds self serving, doesn't it? But it's true. She talks at work all the time about her sexual escapades, especially with her husband. She also confides her displeasure with him. It seems he is not as intelligent as she would like. In fact, he is so blue collar he bores her when he talks.

This revelation comes from a woman who is not God's gift to higher reasoning. She has ideas and thoughts and creative tendencies, but she is no Rhodes Scholar. Tim is a welder by trade. He works hard with his hands both on the job and with her.

Gentleness became one of the areas that tweaked my interest my third day on the job with her. She mentioned the fact that she wanted a softer touch. I like soft touch. I could do this. These thoughts raced through my brain. I am a smart guy. I like creative endeavors. I could make love to her the way she wants it.

So is that it? Is it ego? Is the answer that shallow? Or is it even shallower. Is it that I am twenty one years old and my hormones are whacked out? Is it that I'm a virgin? Is it that Marilyn won't put out even after four years?

What kind of future do I think I'll have with this woman? She is married to a man who'd most likely beat the shit out of me if he found out I screwed his wife. She wouldn't leave him anyway. What I'm hoping to do is probably the most reckless, stupid move I've ever performed in my life.

Is that it? Is it the thrill of danger and recklessness? Am I in search of a thrill I can no longer get from sneaking off with Marilyn and stripping her down and having all the fun one can have without consummation?

I stare at this Playboy Bunny vision on my bed. She is leaning back, propped up on her elbows. Her cantaloupe breasts rise and fall as she looks at the colored lights on my ceiling. Her feet are kicking slightly, lending her a little-girl-lost appearance. Every twenty-one-year-old's dream.

Why should I pass this up? She would keep her mouth shut. I would get something I really want, and maybe we would do it again. And again. And again.

Is that it? Is it the lure of illicit sex in an ongoing setting? Is my libido so high one woman is not enough?

I love Marilyn. I know I do. But does that mean I can't love anyone else? Do I have to compartmentalize my love, such as; I love Marilyn for life, I love Cindi for pure sex, I love Margo for creative talent, I love Terry for how she treats me.

Cindi is tantalizing. The more I watch her, the more I want to stop thinking and just get to it. I am afraid I'll talk myself out of this. I mean, how many times is a luscious blond going to knock on my door crying and within ten minutes send me signals that I can have her if I want. And boy, do I ever want.

Is she fulfilling a desire in me I can't get quenched elsewhere? Is that it? What drives this desire anyway? Is it my low self-esteem? Is it my under-appreciation of who I am and what I have to offer? Is it something that will last me the rest of my entire life? Will there be other Cindi's that come along and fill this desire?

I am nervous. Why wouldn't I be? I am about to potentially wreck my engagement because of a crying, hot to trot, blond acquaintance. Am I a gambler? Do I need the thrill of competition to fuel my life?

Ultimately, I have to do something. I have some really nice, soft music massaging us both between the temples. That is where the best sex takes place. Sex is not so much a physical act as a mental one. An emotional one. If you are only physically invested, your payoff is going to be limited.

I have talked with Cindi for three months and I have formed an emotional bond with her. I agree her husband can be an oaf (but that doesn't seem to stop her when he has her upside down with her legs over his shoulders). Naked. I also like the way she flirts. I like the way I flirt when she flirts. Have I mentioned she's drop-dead gorgeous?

I know, I know. I just mentioned how shallow the physical aspect is, but attached to that physical aspect is fantasy. When you combine those two items the whole equation runs amuck somewhat like one of Einstein's chalkboard rabbit trails.

She is a fantasy. Hugh Hefner would want this woman in his harem. Have I not dreamed of this woman in this situation since I was eleven or twelve years old? Of course I have. Can I help it that fate, the gods, my dumb luck timed this in the middle of my engagement to Marilyn?

Is that it? Am I upset that I never got the 'fling' I always wanted and now that it's here and available I'm going to take advantage of the opportunity? I realize, of course, that all these questions truly strike at the heart of the truth. They all contain an aspect of my dilemma. I am unsure whether I have the strength of character to do the 'right thing'.

There are many men who would tell me to go for it. There are even a few women who would as well (especially those women in my family that don't care too much for my fiancée). This is a decision that rests solely on my shoulders.

I read a quote by Robin Williams the other day. It said, "In all God's infinite wisdom He gave men a head and a penis and only enough blood use one at a time." Ain't it the truth? Is that crass? Yes. Is it true? Yes.

She's going to get impatient soon. I have to do something. I know what I want to do and I know what I need to do and I don't have a clue as to what to do. I sound insane. Temporary insanity? Now I'm going to look for excuses? No, if I do this, it will be with a sense of responsibility.

I may not fess up to it on my own, but I won't try to lie my way out of the consequences either. Oh, so this is supposed to make me appear to be a better person? Sounds like a chicken shit person to me.

I don't suppose it would be a good thing to walk up to your fiancée and say, "Hi babe. I just screwed Cindi while you were at work. I really enjoyed it, but since she's married with two children and all, I don't think it will happen again. Hey, but I got a lot of questions answered."

I am sure I would need to duck before I got too far into that monologue. Is that it? Am I just afraid and looking for a way out? Would that be the easy way to say, "I'm not sure marriage is for me?" Is that the way I really feel?

I think I want to be married. In fact, I am pretty sure of it. But truly, how can one tell until he's actually done it? And then, is it not too late? I don't suppose a 'trial marriage' will be in vogue within the next six months.

Living together is what some people call that. But there is something a bit less than marriage there. That knot is not tied with the inseparable connotation that a marriage certificate owns. Living together is tying a bow tie in your tennis shoes. You can always just pull one string and it comes undone nicely.

A marriage is a complex knot that requires lawyers, family and friends to work through if you wish to undo it. Is that it? Am I afraid of being married? To the wrong person? Is Cindi more the 'right' person? Is that what I want to find out?

Earlier, when she first came in, we stood in hallway talking. She went on about Tim and their latest spat. The drink in my hand had become old. I delayed getting closer to her for three centuries or three minutes, take your pick. One guess as to how long it feels to me.

Somewhere I discovered the nerve to hug her. Oh god what a smile. Her teeth are perfectly straight, unlike mine. Mine aren't so much crooked but compared to hers they are.

Her voice is deep and soft. "Thank you. You've been so nice to me. I know you weren't ready to listen to a ditzy blond cry on your shoulder tonight."

That was really nice, holding her in my arms while she cried. She snuggled up nice and tight too. "Anytime. That's what friends are for."

She strolls into my bedroom while I hit the kitchen and throw together a drink. I hear her sigh. The sound resembles the inviting, soft, swirling whoosh of a warm spring breeze.

"This is really good." She cradles the Sloe Gin Fizz in the palm of her hand. I sit down beside her. On the bed.

"You aren't having one?"

"No, I don't drink very often."

"That's one of the things I like about you. You keep your head on straight all the time unlike Tim. He'd have about ten beers down his throat by now."

I don't particularly like talking about her husband right now. I want to focus on her. "You can kick off your shoes and get comfortable if you like." I feel bold saying that but safe enough that I'm not appearing over-anxious.

She uses her toes to push her Reeboks off at the heels. "Don't mind if I do." She sets the drink on my nightstand. "So, do you have any suggestions?"

My mind is racing like electrons in an open current. I don't want to come up with anything that even resembles her husband, any answers that might help them or anything that directs her attention to anything but me.

So I kiss her.

I watch as her sculpted lashes fall, thin black feathers landing gently on the tops of her cheeks. Her tongue is warm and thrilling and patient. I don't want to be patient, but I know I have to be, especially since I want this moment to last forever.

No, not the sex to come, not the explosive high we look forward to or dream of. I just want this kiss to last for eternity. This model, goddess, diva, whatever, has condescended to kiss me. That she would do this is beyond all imagining. I could not dream this. Ever.

The actual contact is validation. It places a seal of authenticity on fantasy. Her lips, silken pillow crescents sliding ever so slowly against mine justify all the dreams I have ever held in my treasure chest of hopes that I store deep in my soul. I like myself because she likes me enough to kiss me.

Sounds lame, to be sure, but it's true. And is that so bad? Women have been known to feel this way for millennia. Many women have justified their existence on less than this.

We fall backward into the bed. She opens those ocean-blue eyes and I want to drown. I dive into them, searching and probing like our tongues a moment ago. There is nothing sexier in this world than the intimate look into another's eyes. No flesh, no tease, no touch can ever match the erotic, sensual power of the eye.

Without breaking my gaze, I lift a shaking left hand up to the fourth button of her blouse and fumble with it. Her eyes open slightly wider revealing controlled excitement that compels me to move faster.

I refuse. I work on the fifth button, this time more deft of hand and less speed.

The slower pace triggers something in her eyes and with little warning I find her lips on mine and her eyes wide open. I dance a slow tango with her tongue and I feel her body press a little tighter against me.

Is this the end of my life? Can I go forward, having attained this dream, with any real sense of there being anything more enticing to come? What am I thinking? We haven't even arrived at our destination yet and I am thinking life can't get any better.

I withdraw from our kiss and her eyes. I look at how her blouse has fallen back to her shoulder and how her bra has a clasp begging to be set free. Being the noble gent that I am, I flick the clasp away from its purpose and release the treasures it had bound.

Ok, so life can get better.

I am so lost now. My face wanders around in slow, bewildered dementia. My tongue decides to leave traces of its travels so that it may find its way back to its starting point or some such nonsense. I feel her hands plunge to her waist. A snap and zip later she is wiggling out of her jeans as my tongue finds the crest of a mountain.

Within minutes we are making love and I now know that life can truly get better. At one picturesque moment, a snapshot burns into my brain. She is riding high, throwing her silver hair to nonexistent breezes and grinding me into sexual oblivion. She is as beautiful in all her ecstatic glory as anything I will ever see again.

Now I know why I shouldn't have done this. At the moment I don't care. All I want now is culmination. Completion. But not until she's ready. I want her to have the ride of her life. She slows and bends down over me, her hair tickling my face. She presses against me and buries a kiss into my mouth that spits a fire only hinted at before.

This is a kiss that expects more. It has all the earmarks of demanding stamina and stalwart dedication to her pleasure. I sense I could be in trouble and I latch onto her hips and stop the motion. I stop everything but the kiss.

We're frozen like two flesh statues. Our tongues curl. Serpentine. A slow-motion dance limited to one small alcove of space.

She tightens around me. I feel goose bumps grow on her arms as my right hand lands with a soft, light touch on her breast. Her eyelids open ever so gentle. Her eyes, such an intense blue, appear glazed with fiery ice.

Her trance fixates on something. Something deep. Something primal.

I raise my left hand to her right breast and squeeze one micrometer at a time. Her personal presence in those incredible eyes diminishes. My fingers find her nipple. She retreats in her eyes further like a woman falling into a well.

With the movement of a ninja, silent, unseen, my hands fill up with her hips. I swirl my own hips clockwise. Slow. Steady. I swim down the vortex of the well, still vibrant in her eyes as they grow wider.

She bolts upright. Her back arches. A shudder, gentle as an earthquake, travels up her body from our connected cores. She now trembles. Constantly. For hours. Or seconds. Or an eternity.

She glares down from on high in one tantalizing moment. She's lost from her eyes. Her vacant stare reveals the crossover from fantasy and exertion to reality. I thrust hard and deep and she screams.

I'm met with a retaliation of hip swirling and nail gouging and breasts pressed into me and a kiss that damn near steals my breath and I join her with my own primal growls.

The world, my house, my room, my body all wink out. The only object of existence rides the waves atop me. I know nothing. I desire nothing. I am nothing.

I don't know how long this lasts. I don't know how I come back to earth, much less to my bedroom and my bed. All I know is a peace and a conviction that we just reached the pinnacle of life has overtaken my soul.

I am engaged to Marilyn but I am in Cindi. On my bed. I do realize why this should never have happened. Now, all I want is more.

Cindi lifts her head as if it weighs a ton. My shoulder feels bare as though it had worn her face and hair like clothing. Her eyes mist like the morning waters of the Caribbean. They meet mine with a soft intensity I've never experienced.

"Oh my God! I...we... are going to have to do this again."

All I can say is, "Kiss me..."

The Continuing Adventures of Rumpald Forskan

"Where the hell is Wanda when you need her?" Captain Rumpald Forskan tossed his breather in the general direction of his disheveled bed.

"Looks like she's been here if you ask me." Ackan sneered at his captain's disapproval.

"If we don't get this piece of crap online and winging to Centauri within the next solar day, we'll be grounded for at least six months."

"No worries. If you like, we can launch now and I'll finish the repairs in flight. I'll only lose a week or so of down time."

"You can't continue to age out on me, Ack. The last time you pulled that trick we ended up off course by an entire parsec and nearly ran out of fuel correcting once the crew thawed."

"Look, don't I always get us there? Almost doesn't count unless it involves almost making it. I can do this."

Rum glanced over the tussled sheets. A wistful gleam shadowed his eyes for a moment before he bellowed into the con, "Ms. Goudtyme! Report to Rec Room One immediately!" Rump shoved his way past his mechanic.

"My my. Getting bolder with your trysts these days aren't you Rump?"

The captain's feet gripped the floor in a dead stop while his body nearly tumbled forward. He turned slightly and glared Ackan's direction. "Watch your mouth. No one's indispensable on this ship other than me."

"Yeah, and Wanda Goudtyme." The captain appeared confused for a moment. "Better hurry, someone may get there before you. I'd hate for you to be second in line…"

Wanda loved dry-dock. Gravity is set at a minimum. Her boobs stand perky and young again. Better yet, her feet felt more pampered than abused. Her body took much less of a pounding screwing around too.

"What's not to love?" she asked the digital mirror.

"Please phrase your question to fit the demeanor of a mirror."

"Who programs your shit personality you digital liar?"

"Ackan Doudis programs all functioning apps on this ship," both Wanda and the mirror state, followed in unison with, "and The Dude disavows even glancing at anything that doesn't work"

Wanda enhanced the curve of her lips ever so slightly. The captain heats up immediately when she takes the time to do this.

The door behind her explodes into a full-charging Captain Rumpald Forskan, his shirt halfway off before he pins her to the wall. "I thought I told you to meet me in my stateroom."

Rump was an interesting specimen. Over six foot tall, she never knew if he kept himself in such good shape by working out in the rec rooms or on top of women. He never seemed to meet one he didn't like. "Well, Rumpy-baby. If you'd keep that damned mechanic of yours out of our hair I might ride you to Alpha Centauri and back.”

“We’d age out,” he stated. His right hand harshly cradled her throat and his breath fell hot across her lips.

“What a way to go, eh?”

“Dammit Wanda, why do you say things like that? You know it makes a man crazy out here.” He slightly loosened his grip on her throat and slipped his lips gently across hers.

“If I don’t drive you crazy, you won’t be sane enough to get us where we’re going. I’m just doing my part.”

“Well, do your part quickly because I have to be on deck in 10. I’m letting Ackan repair while we’re in down time.”

“Rump. The last time you did that we almost croaked.”

“C’mon. Times a wastin’.”

Wanda tugged on the zipper between her breasts. Her entire outfit fell to the floor in a silken avalanche of silence.

If horny idiots grew on trees Rumpald Forskan would be the low hanging fruit…

***

Hypersleep never woke well. Blurred vision, atrophied muscles despite the massagers which ran constantly during the years of travel.

The Captain checked star charts while everyone else groaned and complained. He always rose a week before anyone else so that he would appear unaffected by the dormancy. The trick was to rise out of the cryotube at the same time as everyone else.

Something was amiss with the charts. None of the star systems matched up with any known coordinates in his computer. He shifted to his black market ops system to see if anything popped up.

"What's up Rumpy? Why the forlorn face?"

Wanda's midrift top didn't quite cover her breasts. The curvature underneath the tattered hem caught his attention more than the screen. "We should run off to my stateroom for a quick one Wanda."

"Whoa. Dial it back. Get everything done first. You act like you haven't had any for years!"

"I'll say it again Wanda. Even though it feels like we just went to sleep yesterday, the testosterone builds up over the years. I'm horny and can't think straight."

"Get us docked and I'll take care of you Sweetie."

"Damnable woman," the Captain muttered as he glanced at a glaring red-winking light on his screen while Wanda strutted away. "Ah shit!"

Wanda spun around and headed back to the Captain. "What's up?"

"We're about 5 parsecs off."

"What the hell?"

"ACKEN DOUDIS!" the Captain screamed into the ship-wide com.

Wanda scuttled away. The Captain could get unpleasant when sufficiently pissed off.

The mechanic arrived at a wobbly trot. "Your Liege."

"Don't "Your Liege" me you little shit! What the hell did you do to navigation this time? I told you to stay clear of that console."

"C'mon Rump! You said you wanted to get there fast, get the shit unloaded, and move on. I took care of it all while you slept. I talked a couple of the guys to giving up a little time. The cargo is dropped, your bank account is fat, and we should be at one of the most amazing vacation planets in the known universes."

"This is a restricted zone. We're not even allowed down there!"

"I rigged the log books to show us on the other side of this galaxy at Minums 7. No one will know…"

"You can't keep doing this you know. One day we'll get caught and my license will be confiscated. This better not be like the last one. We lost two crew and a ton of credits."

"Cap'n, the brochure said this place has the potential to blow your mind."

"I just hope that's figurative and not literal."

"Look. You said you wanted something different. You also cannot afford to be brain-scanned if we're caught and show any knowledge of the programming. I'm not a navigator. They'd never suspect me. We're good."

"Many more of the "accidental destination" reports and they'll start digging deeper. Nothing to do now but go check it out, eh?"

"After you!"

***

The Captain, Acken, Wanda, and two buxom officers, Nym Fo – communications and Randy Gurll – first officer, flew the shuttle from spacedock into the domed city planetside. The pic on the brochure did not do the place justice. All planetfall tourists were required to check in at this one location. The city bustled with excited men and women. Conversations flew in many languages other than Galactic, some familiar, some not.

The Captain surveyed everything. He noticed dress patterns and lack thereof. Apparently this planet was a bawdy playground because all manner of provocative dress flew across his straining eyes. He liked what his eyes gifted him.

"Ok Acken. This looks to be just what the Captain ordered."

"Hey, my sources don't lie. They tell me there is no place better to get laid in three universes."

They stepped up to the concierge's floating desk. "Newbies, eh? How did you hear about us?"

"How did you know?" the Captain asked.

"Droll. Uniform. Really? Only newbies would expose themselves to the tortures of this place. Better to act like the locals. Your entourage came better prepared, yet still too understated. Just beware your first few hours may be difficult," the attendant explained.

"Difficult?" the Captain, Wanda, and Acken asked simultaneously.

"At least you know to be concerned. We get so many ridiculous day trippers who think they can handle everything. Once you walk outside this dome, you may "get" and "do" most anything you can imagine."

"Oh, Cap'n can imagine quite a bit," Acken interjected.

"This is a bit more complex. The Dome acts as a suppressor of the power of thought. Once you step outside, you will be subjected to your imagination. What you picture in your thoughts will become what or who you are. Once you're out there, you cannot come back into the dome area for 12 earth hours. Your maximum time is 48 earth hours. Make the most of them."

"What?" again in unison.

"By telling you this, I am already setting you on your journey. You would have arrived at the answer about the quirks of this planet eventually, but we've had people go mad before they figure out the issue. Just remember this one rule – whatever you think not only affects you on a feeling level. On a visual and physical level, a certain amount of reality can be altered. Be careful. You're here to have fun..." he stated and walked his desk toward the next person.

"That's all pretty vague isn't it?" Wanda searched for anything on the attendant's face which would grant them more insight as to what would happen once they headed outside. It was the unknown which scared the crap out of her.

No response. They'd been summarily dismissed.

"Pow wow," the Captain stated. The three women and Acken formed a circle with their leader. "Ok, what we think will internally affect us from a feeling perspective, but also visually and physically. Let's find out what that means. Randy and Nym, you're with me."

"Shouldn't we speculate a little before we step out? Acken asked.

"What fun is there in that? Let's just dive in and see what happens," the Captain responded.

The six of them headed out the door. As they passed the final gate, the attendant repeated to each person going through, "Remember. Once you step back into the dome, you will not be allowed back out for one week. You cannot gain reentry into the dome for 12 Earth hours." The attendant droned the same mantra over and over to those walking out.

They cleared the door into a slightly bluer planet than he'd expected. He always expected green because the earth foliage predominantly grew green. The Captain turned to Wanda who was making mischievous eyes at Acken.

"Wanda. Save yourself for me until I'm done with these two."

"Shithead." Wanda stated flatly.

Nym cried out in alarm and stepped away from the Captain.

"What the fuck?" the Captain spewed out as he worked to control his mind.

Acken and Wanda doubled over in laughter and revulsion. The Captain's head waffled back and forth from the handsome, chiseled face they'd all known for years, to a swirling pile of shit with eyes, ears, mouth, and nose. The Captain's voice came out mushy and slurred.

"Dickhead!" Acken shouted at him. Immediately, his head reshaped itself, drooping and unnerving. Laughter exploded from his five shipmates.

Wanda strutted up to the Captain. She gently stroked his slumped head and whispered seductively, "Oh Forskan. How manly you look today."

Immediately, the Captains crown literally stiffened and pointed straight to the sky. His phallic head reddened and shimmered back and forth between this apparition and his normal feature, albeit an enraged version of his normally calm and placid self.

Acken fell over laughing, to which Nym shouted at him, "Dumbass!" Immediately Acken morphed into a glaze-eyed donkey, braying at nothing in particular, although the brays resembled laughter.

Once back under control, the Captain shouted, "Listen up!" The command carried a note of demand and authority. His crew snapped back quickly, including Acken, to a wary, potentially under siege unit. The Captain's tone conveyed urgency. Acken fought off a desire to lapse back into laughter.

"Captain. Apparently when someone directly describes another, a visual anomaly occurs. The anomaly, though, is not solely relegated to visual and I knew and felt my transformation to a burro."

"No shit Sherlock," the Captain retorted. He realized his mistake too late as his ship's mechanic now possessed a hat and magnifying glass, seemingly of ancient origin.

Acken regained control of his personal perception. "Captain, when you made the "sleuth" suggestion, my mind went to my perception of the character. Once I regained a more neutral mindset, I returned to my regular form. My conjecture at this point is that if one can maintain a neutral mindset and refuse to take on another's suggestion, he or she may successfully win back their generally accepted appearance."

"Isn't this the same shi---, uh, stuff the gentleman told us before we stepped out?" Wanda asked.

"It's one thing to be told something, another to actually experience it you brazen nymphomaniac," Acken parried. Wanda slipped into the visage of a wanton woman and began groping the Captain, going straight for his groin.

Wanda fought for control. Her biggest issue was that she didn't want to stop. Acken's laughter jerked her out of the scenario. "Dumb fuck!" she blurted Acken's direction.

Acken immediately began ramming what once was his head into the nearby wall. After a couple thrusts, Nym and the Captain pulled him back. Soon he was holding his head with a pained look on his face.

"Listen up!" the Captain shouted, this time furious. "We either get ourselves under control, or we'll never get back in the dome. This planet may not be all the fun and games it appears to be."

Acken's face sobered. "We're actually trapped here for the next 12 hours. I hope Boonie and the crew don't allow anything stupid on board. What if the "Dome" people have learned to channel the planet effects? Could spell trouble if the ship's compliment gets taken unaware."

"My thoughts exactly. I swear on the Romulan Nebula if we get out of this, your ass is mine!"

Acken jerked around, pants dropped, and began backing into the Captain. "Shit!" Acken barked and the Captain recoiled from the brown projectile headed his way.

"What the hell…!"

As quickly as the moment happened, everything snapped back to the five of them standing in a circle. The women snickered and the Captain scowled at Acken.

"Hey, it wasn't my fault! You need to keep your potty mouth under control…"

The Captain's head took on the shape of an old-time toilet. When he spoke, the lid flapped up and down like a cross between a board and a soft tortilla. "Dammit Acken, keep your mind straight!"

"Captain," Acken stated as the toilet seat fell back into the scowling face of his boss. "When you called me that name a moment ago, you know, the one about my backside…" Again, his backside flashed toward the Captain for an instant. "I'm sure it appeared to everyone as though I turned around to point my backside to you, yet from my point of view, I still faced you. Everything was illusion, yet I felt what was happening to me."

"Even the projectile?" Wanda asked.

"Yes, that felt real enough. I wonder. If I hadn't got my mind under control again, would you have been splattered?"

"Ooo. Let's not go there," Nym stated as she crinkled her face.

"We have to," Captain Forskan interjected. "Randy, we haven't heard from you on any of this. What's your assessment of the situation? Are we solely in danger from our own minds, or is our ship at risk?"

His first officer pursed her lips in the same fashion that had landed her the position months ago. "At the risk of saying something I'll regret, I didn't sign up for this. I thought Nym and I were coming planetside to ride the Captain and grab a little girl time once he passed out."

Three naked bodies writhed in unison on the ground for more than an uncomfortable ten seconds before the three of them regained composure, the last one snapping out of it being Randy.

"Holy…" Acken began.

"Whew!" Wanda exclaimed wiping her brow in mock lightheadedness.

"What did you feel?" Randy asked Nym. "Did you feel him inside you?"

"Uh, I was on his face. If you're talking tongue, hell yeah!" Nym crowed.

"Interesting. I was on his face as well. And I felt it. All the right spots Captain," Randy coyly threw his direction. "The point is, we felt it, right?"

"Interesting. You both had me on my back. That's not what I experienced." The Captain stroked his light beard in contemplation. "What about you Wanda?"

"Oh, I went straight to girl time…" she smiled weakly.

"Me too!" Acken interjected. "Only problem was, I couldn't insert myself into the mix…"

"Really?" Wanda exclaimed. "Me neither."

"Neither of you were in the original suggestion," Randy observed.

A group of men headed their direction from the nearby woods. Their appearance waffled between confident and desperate.

"Captain…" Acken muttered.

"I see them. Wanda, Randy. Right and left flanks. Acken on point. Nym, you and I are on Acken. Focus on the five of us being a starship battle cruiser. On my mark, detach as stealth attack craft. I want them disabled, not dead, if possible. We're vulnerable until we figure this thing out. I want to see what they've got though"

The approaching party of seven stopped at ten paces. "We don't want no trouble. We just need your passes to get back in the dome," the lithe, muscular leader stated flatly.

"That's not going to happen," the Captain said as he nodded his flanks to advance.

The leader looked at Randy and said, "Aren't you the sweet little tulip? What do you think Derringer? Clip her petals?"

Randy morphed into a tall, breeze-wavered flower while one of the leader's men became a large, sharp pair of scissors and snipped at the First Officer.

"Acken! You're my Rock n Roll!" The engineer smashed into the scissors with incredible force just as they nicked one of Randy's leaf stems. Randy reformed clutching a bloody left bicep while Derringer's legs crumpled underneath him with Acken straddling the injured man.

"Watch me slap the snot out of this guy Captain!" Acken bellowed as he slapped the leader so viciously mucous flew from his nostrils.

"Stop! Stop! I give! I give!" the leader shouted as he struggled to regain composure under Acken's beating.

The leader doubled over when Acken backed off, but the Captain grabbed the man's neck in his right hand and pinned him against the dome wall. "One reason why I don't break your neck like a dried twig," the Captain growled.

The man's neck turned into a brittle twig. He struggled to recompose himself under the pressure of the Captains fingers. "Please. Please, "he gasped. "We're desperate. I can help you."

"How," the Captain demanded as he squeezed the man's neck tighter even while it reformed.

"Fighting like this drains your energy. The longer and more real you maintain these illusions, the more you get drained of energy."

"Ok, that's useful," the Captain said as he backed off on his vice grip. "What else you got?"

"It can take days to get your strength back. Every time you morph and actually use what you've morphed into, your system will go into a bit of shock within the next four or five hours. The more drastic the morph, the more exhausted you become. Rock Man here is in for debilitating fatigue soon."

"What happened to your reentry chips? Captain Forskan asked.

"We got ambushed by about ten men and they took ours. We're just a couple families on vacation. These guys were brutal. They killed my son-in-law. We've been stranded out here for weeks."

"Has anyone in your party ever been here before?" asked the Captain.

"No. We just saw the ad and decided we needed some R&R." the leader responded as he rubbed his neck where the Captain had released it from his grip. "This place is billed as the "Pleasure Capital of the Galaxy."

"Anything else?"

The man fidgeted. "Umm…"

"Out with it man, or I'll pulverize you and your entire party and be done with you!"

"If you morph into something non-animate, like, not living, you'll get hit hard by the body's reaction within three hours. We've seen many people die when this happens. Your rock friend will suffer as will my man Derringer who became scissors." The man stared at the ground. "He volunteered to sacrifice himself to help us get out of here."

"What's your name?" the Captain demanded.

"Green," the man replied. Immediately, he turned a deep shade of green.

"Well Green," the Captain released him. "We'll come for you once we get inside. Stay close by though. We may not have time to look more than once for you."

***

"Captain. Apparently, we won't be our strongest anytime past now. With every engagement we run into, our strength will diminish and our chances for returning to the ship will plummet with our strength. The time to force our way back into the dome is now."

Nym stepped back a pace, satisfied with her assessment.

"Agreed," stated the Captain. "We will lay low, avoid contact with others at all costs, and monitor the dome. Whenever someone leaves the dome, they must come out somewhere. There's no trace of the exit we came from, so we must act quick when we see someone. We likely will not get more than one chance. Once they know we're on to them, they will send a team to take care of us."

"I don't even remember how long it took us to step outside once we cleared their gate people," Randy said.

"It wasn't more than a minute. We were so caught up in the "training speech" we likely missed some blatant clues," Wanda added.

"I was intrigued by the opening when we walked out. It appeared the dome was somewhat of an open forum. Remember? We could see the blue forest. It kind of appeared once the last gate person had done their spiel. They must be using some sort of real-time projection in conjunction with an opening device which is both silent and perfectly timed to the illusion that there is no real doorway. From this side, the opening will appear quickly and close just as quickly. Could be no more than a few seconds." Acken leaned back attempting to catch sight of the top of the dome.

"Do you think there's something up top that may help us?" asked the Captain following Acken's gaze.

"Many times in structures like this, there are manhole exits to work on issues pertaining to deterioration of the asset due to weather patterns. I'd be willing to bet we would find a way in up there." Acken squinted in the bright sun.

"They'll be moving on our ship almost immediately. Hopefully they have a backlog since a good number of ships docked just before we did." The Captain's forehead creased. "We must move now."

"How the hell do you propose we get up there?" Wanda asked.

"Nym, you beanstalk you. You're like that Jack and the Beanstalk story kids love to read. I'm sure you're just as stout as the story told," the Captain stated with a grin.

Nym morphed and sprouted up the side of the dome with amazing speed. The Captain, and Acken quickly grabbed onto the rapid-rising stalk and saved themselves significant climbing. Wanda and Randy hesitated and found themselves struggling up the vines once it stopped growing.

On top of the dome, Rump and Acken quickly surveyed the area. They stood on a flat circular surface about 20 meters in diameter. Scuff marks in the accumulated silt showed them a maintenance access door about dead center.

As Randy and Wanda crested the top, Nym began to reform. "Reform your head and arms first Nym!" the Captain shouted. "We don't want you at the bottom of this thing!"

Acken grabbed a clutch of leaves and limbs which morphed into a hand and arms on the edge of the flat surface. Nym's head and torso followed. She began sliding down the curvature on the edge of the dome dragging Acken headlong with her.

Wanda dove for Acken's feet, latched on to them, and began sliding herself. Randy and the Captain each sprinted to the three crewman and each picked up one of Wanda's legs. They tugged and pulled their mates back onto the flat surface.

Nym lay near the edge, ashen-faced and visibly debilitated. "Sorry Captain," Acken said. "I didn't have the strength to hold her."

"The two of you are compromised physically. You'll need to lag behind whatever we do. Otherwise you'll likely get yourselves killed," the Captain advised.

"Captain," Wanda caught his attention. "Since they're telling everyone they must remain outside the dome for twelve hours that must mean they don't project needing more time than that for their nefarious acts."

"We've been out here for about five hours sir," Randy added.

"All the more reason to move quickly. As long as they didn't detect our rapid rise to the top of this damnable thing, and as long as we can get in through this maintenance door, we may be able to get to our ship before they pillage the damned thing." The

Captain examined the door. "How much juice you got in you Acken?"

"I'm sure I could make myself into a key," Acken offered.

"No, not a metallic key. You are already at risk soon for that debilitating hit your body's going to take soon. Green was very specific. You need to morph into something living that can get into the lock and unlock it. How about a very sturdy vine?" the Captain asked.

"That could work. I could trip the tumblers and bypass the need for a key. Or I can snake into the digital morass if I need to by making myself into electrons. I'll give it a shot." Acken sat staring at the lock.

"Why aren't you doing anything?" the Captain asked.

"Maybe he no longer has the strength to morph," Wanda offered.

"No. No. I think I'm lacking a third-party suggestion. Have you noticed we've all morphed off someone else's suggestion? Apparently we cannot morph off our own suggestion." Acken observed.

"Acken, you're a strong, hearty vine," the Captain suggested.

Immediately, Acken morphed and went to work on the lock. Within ten minutes he withdrew all his plant appendages and remorphed into himself. "It should be unlocked Captain." He stated. "By the way, I'm feeling the exhaustion coming on. I don't think I'll be moving from this spot," he stated and collapsed in a heap.

"Nym. See to Acken. Do what you can for him until you start feeling it," the Captain ordered.

"Yes sir." Nym strolled to the engineer and sat lotus style next to him.

"Wanda. Randy. Let's see what we're up against." Without hesitation, the Captain pulled the door up, opening a dark, musty hole which contained rungs built into the walls serving as a ladder.

The three descended into the abyss. Once their eyes grew accustomed to the reduced light, they determined they stood in a circular room five meters in diameter. Opposite the ladder rungs, another door barred their way.

"If this one's locked, I fear Acken won't have the strength to unlock it," Wanda whispered.

The Captain stalked over to the door and pulled the lever. The door opened with a near silent woosh. Ambient lighting splashed the bulkhead. A stairway descended into more light. The Captain strode to the stairway, peered down, then casually walked down the steps like he owned them.

Wanda and Randy followed. At the bottom of the stairs they came to a hallway arcing to the left and right. The captain motioned Wanda and Randy to the left. He signaled 20 paces. He went right. They returned to the stairwell.

Wanda whispered, "There's a series of doors beginning at about 15 paces, all on the left. They have no windows. Could be sleeping quarters."

"I don't think so," whispered the Captain. "Not this high up. I ran into the same thing on my side. Follow me."

At the first door on the Captain's right, he tiptoed past it and signaled Wanda to open it on the count of three. Once he ticked off the three digits on his fingers, the three of them skirted into a room filled with music and the soft laughter of two people in intimate contact.

"Oooh! You're such a naughty snake," the woman cooed as the Captain and his ladies peaked around the wall separating the entrance from what appeared to be a bedroom. The ceiling opened up to a clear sky. Apparently the ceiling was retractable. "Can you hear me in there?" the woman begged. "If you can, arch yourself and spin around. Slow! Slow, slow, slow, slow. That's it! Oh my god!" she shrieked.

The Captain, Wanda, and Randy headed back into the hallway. "Looks like the natives get a little kinky R&R," Randy observed.

"I can't imagine you get up here without some sort of clout. Has to be one of the perks of doing well in their business. I say we go back in and ambush them when they're done. Hopefully they will retract the ceiling once they've finished. I'd much rather fight them on our terms, not their imaginations. I'm sure they're much more used to this planet's unnerving effects on humans." The Captain said in a hushed tone.

"Agreed," said Wanda. "You and Randy should go first. I'm not quite as adept and hand-to-hand as the two of you."

"Let's roll," said Randy as the Captain reopened the door.

"Damn babe," a man's voice carried from the other room. "That snake thing was a great idea. I got a bird's eye view, so to speak."

The sound of a flutter of wings darted around the corner for an instant before the woman exclaimed, "Stop that! You know I'm more susceptible right after and orgasm! Go screw yourself you mangina!"

Curious, Wanda poked her head around the corner in time to catch sight of a penis curved back and penetrating its own base. The man snapped back to himself and slammed a hand against the wall. "I told you to never fucking do that to me again!"

The ceiling began retracting. "Hey, you started it asshole!" Momentarily the man's shape shifted and abruptly returned to its original form when the ceiling silently locked into place.

Before either one of them could gather themselves, the Captain attacked the man, diving across the woman and catching him square on the chin with the base of his hand. The woman whirled around to her left only to meet Randy's roundhouse punch to the woman's left cheek.

"Damn that shit hurts!" Randy exclaimed.

"I'm sure she got the worst of that," Wanda observed. Looks like you broke her jaw.

Within seconds, the two were subdued, tied up and gagged with their own clothing which the invaders had been ripped into appropriate tethers. The captives were tied to chairs to keep them from activating the ceiling. The Captain had located a couple sharp knives in the small kitchen.

"I'm only asking once before I start cutting on you, so pay attention. Do you understand there will be no second question?" The two prisoners nodded.

The Captain motioned Randy to ungag the man. "How do we get to the control center of this place?"

"Fuck you," the man spat at the Captain. Captain Rumpald brought down his knife and impaled the top of the man's hand between the bones of the forefinger and middle finger. The man screamed. Wanda shot a worried glance at the door.

The Captain motioned the man be muffled again. "Soundproofed," the Captain explained to Wanda's fearful gaze. She visibly relaxed. "Your turn," the Captain growled as he pointed his bloodied blade at her left eye.

Her undeniable panic stilled to her nodding a resigned affirmation of her predicament. The Captain motioned Wanda to ungag the woman. "Where is the control center?"

"As you're walking to the right outside in the hallway, it's the only door on the left," she whimpered.

"Good. Good. Now, for the life-saving answer of the day, how heavily guarded is this room?" The Captain wagged the knife from one eye to the other.

"None. None. There's no one but the main controller in there," she stammered.

"Key card required?"

The woman shook her head no.

"I can simply walk in?" The woman nodded. "I sincerely doubt that." Wanda gagged her again and the Captain grabbed her by the throat and stood her up. "Wanda, stay here with him. If we don't return within five minutes, kill him and proceed with plan B."

From behind the two prisoners, Wanda's eyes flickered in confusion for a moment before she grasped she would be on her own if the Captain and Randy were not successful in commandeering the Control Room. She nodded.

The captive, the Captain, and Randy strolled to the door on the left which led to the Control Room. A retina-scan device was imbedded into the door on the left-hand side. The woman attempted to squint her eyes shut. Randy pulled at the top and bottom of her right eye while the captain pressed his knife into her abdomen, slowly impaling her. Her eyes shot wide open for a moment and the door silently opened with the minutest of breaths.

"Gotta love top shelf technology," the Captain muttered as he rushed through the door searching out a target. Randy shoved the bleeding, writing woman through the door, smearing blood along the wall as they entered.

A woman walked out of what appeared to be a restroom in time to catch Rumpald's fist with her face. She reeled backward, her head striking the metal wall with tremendous force. She crumpled to the ground, unconscious. The door shut behind them.

"Tie both of them up. Make the ties painful. Then have Wanda get Acken and Nym if they're able to move. Then get back here and cover the door. Block the door open when you leave so I don't have to keep sticking this woman with my knife. Make it quick because I'll be vulnerable until you return."

"Yes Captain," Randy acknowledged while Rumpald strolled over to the controls.

The Captain found the communications module and hailed his ship.

"Acting Captain Doggle. Any word on our missing party?" Boone's face appeared on the monitor. "Captain!"

"No time Boonie. This planet's a trap. Have they attempted to board us yet?"

"They're docking now, Captain."

"Detain them surgically. I don't want them warning anyone planetside. Deadly force if necessary."

"Aye, Captain." Doggle barked orders for a few minutes, then returned to the screen. "Are you in need of help?"

"We're holding our own for now. Just get my ship out of orbit and away from this hellhole. Don't send a team to rescue us. Either we get off this planet on our own or you just inherited the ship Mr. Doggle. Do you understand me?"

"Aye, Captain. How long do I give you?" Concern creased Doggle's forehead.

"If we don't contact you within six hours, I'm sure we won't be worth returning for. I will upload a report as soon as possible while we have the Control Room. I'm sure we won't be able to hold this long. If we don't make it, get this report to the proper authorities. I'm sure you'll know what to do Boonie."

"I'm counting on hearing from you Captain. I'm going to go oversee the alien ship and its complement. Once the ground does not hear from them, you know you will lose your element of surprise which I surmise you currently enjoy."

"Well assessed, Boonie. Get to it. I've got to cover the door until the rest of my team gets here."

"Aye Captain."

They both switched off the communication. Rumpald stepped over the unconscious woman and perused the one bleeding on the chair. He shook his head and waited.

After a few minutes, he heard a clamor from the stairwell. He poked his head out the door propped open by a chair. Randy had Nym draped across her shoulders and was using the smooth wall to help slide her forward toward the Control Room. Soon, behind her, Wanda was dragging Acken, apparently unconscious, by his hands.

Once Randy and Nym crossed the threshold, the Captain scurried out to help Wanda. They carried Acken in overtop the chair, then released the door from its obstruction.

"Have they caught on yet?" Wanda queried.

"No, but we just made it. Boonie was being boarded when I hailed him. We don't have much time. What about those two?"

"They're going to be major liabilities. I did notice a medical room, at least it had the markings on the door. I think we should take a look," Randy interjected.

"Take Randy. Make it quick. Two minutes max."

"Will do."

As the women exited the control room, the communications alert sounded. The signal originated from the ship's ID, so Captain Forskan opened the viewer. Boone's face appeared.

"All secured Captain. I estimate you'll have no more than 10 minutes before they catch on to us. Orders?"

"Send a team in gunboat. Two gunners, a pilot and two musclemen. We have two incapacitated crew members. We will make our way to the top of the dome. This must be a tactical, surgical operation. We won't get a second shot at it. Rendezvous in twenty-seven minutes." The Captain rubbed his forehead with his right index finger.

Boone nodded to someone off-screen. "Done Captain. I can tell this does not look good. Plan B?" Boone queried.

"If you do not hear from me once we board the gunboat or 30 minutes, whichever comes first, get the hell out of here. Remember to monitor our emergency frequency. We only use that frequency if I initiate it. Otherwise, presume us dead and run. These folk will come after you."

"Roger that." Boone reached to cut communication, then hesitated. "Been a pleasure Captain."

"Back atcha Boonie. Take care of my ship."

Both men severed communication simultaneously. Wanda and Randy returned with what looked like helmets. They contained a clear visor which wrapped around the head and contained what appeared to be a microphone and speakers.

"We found these charging up in the med-room. Since they appear to be made of material similar to the dome, we thought they might come in handy once we're outside," Wanda reported.

"Good work ladies. Randy, you and Wanda take Acken, I got Nym. Back to the roof. We have 22 minutes to get up there and get out of here. Locate any weapons?" the Captain asked.

Randy tossed him what appeared to be a stun gun. "We get overrun, this won't help at all, but at least it's something."

The Captain slung Nym across his left shoulder and held the gun in his right hand. "Get him up top. I'll follow. If the gunboat gets there and I don't, you need to go. No waiting. We may have already been discovered." The Captain stared both women down. "Understood?"

"Aye," they muttered as they lifted the engineer and headed for the stairwell.

At the base of the stairwell, the Captain said, "Fifteen minutes to get topside. I'll hold here until you get Acken topside. Come back and let me know once you've got him up."

The women grunted with their load and hustled up the stairs.

Nym moaned quietly as the Captain shifted her weight to a less strenuous position. He noted a flashing red reflection on the curved walls of the hallway. He backed closer to the stairs. Another, darker reflection moved in silken silence. He aimed the gun at the door.

The shadow hesitated, then darted. The captain pulled the trigger, held a moment, and then pulled the trigger again. A laser weapon slid across the floor. The man who once held it lie crumpled and groaning in a heap.

The Captain dropped Nym with a thunk. He sprinted to the weapon. As he snatched it from the ground, he somersaulted into the hallway. A slightly injured woman fumbled with her weapon.

The Captain triggered the stun gun again. She fell in a heap, her weapon sliding away from him down the hall. He cursed. Footsteps. Many footsteps from both directions.

He sprinted back to Nym. He checked the time. They still had ten minutes before the rescue ship arrived. Randy and Wanda were nowhere in sight. He lifted Nym's dead weight and took the stairs two at a time, both weapons cradled under his right arm.

At the hatch, Wanda and Randy reached for Nym from above. Once they had her arms, they lifted her. The Captain holstered the stun gun in his pants, whirled and trained the laser on the stairwell.

He winged the first man around the corner who fell back into the next couple people behind him. Tumbling bodies met the Captain's ears as he scrambled up the ladder. He dove off the top rung onto the roof of the dome as numerous shots whizzed past.

Randy slammed the door shut. Without a word, they worked to get their friends ready to be loaded on the gunboat.

"I'm gonna kick Acken's ass when he comes to," the Captain muttered.

Wanda and Randy grinned. They knew better.

All three kept shooting pensive glances to the sky as they awaited the first head to show itself from the door.

Michael's Writing Challenge

While sci-fi is my reading passion, I am not comfortable writing the genre yet. I own a strong desire to write sci-fi but I have not mustered the kahuna's to do so.

Humor also challenges me. Writing something funny which makes people laugh would be great. I've tried my hand at "funny writing" before and I must say, I'm not quite sure about my ability to do so. However, that said, I laughed my ass off writing the first installment of "The Continuing Adventures of Rumpald Forskan."

A late addition to this book is a second short story titled "Conflict of Interest." The story is a vignette I started writing fifteen or twenty years ago. My challenge here was to pick up where I left off and see what happens. I ended up enjoying the process of writing both stories. I may possibly launch into my sci-fi-writing dream now...

About the Author

Michael Ray King is a five-time Royal Palm Literary Award winning author. Michael has ten published books and is a "Book Whisperer" which is someone who coaches writers on how to get their story out into written words.

Michael is currently working on three book projects. One book is poetry (as yet untitled), one a dark-humor/sci-fi titled *The Continuing Adventures of Rumpald Forskan* based on the short story contained in this book, and lastly the book *Inking Your Thinking – The Mindset of Writing*.

Michael's Writing Sites:

www.MichaelRayKing.com

www.PoetryinBlackandWhite.com

www.TheInspiredMicUS.com

www.FictionsFootsteps.Wordpress.com

www.MichaelRayKingPublishing.com

Amazon Author Page –Michael Ray King

Excerpts from Michael's books

The Method Writers

"C'mon Jess. This is crazy. I didn't marry you and every pervert in the county." I scratch the back of my head, conscious that every time I do this, she yells at me. I know what I need to do. I need to send my wife packing. Yet I want to cling to the ridiculous hope that she'll stop sleeping around. I glare into the mirror at the stupid look splayed across my face.

"Dolores, we should go." A twenty-something man delivers the statement like I pissed in his soup.

"Yes, Dolores. Listen to your husband." I try for condescending but fear the words sound petty.

Laughter bangs against the walls like a crazed pinball. "Husband?" the redhead chides. "Hell, I just met these two an hour ago." She brushes back a stray hair from her face and cups Jessica's right breast. "You can go, Harry, I'm not quite done here."

Jessica studies me like a lab rat, a trace of pity in her glance, then she locks into a wet kiss with Dolores.

Writing is Easy (from the short story Lavender Hour)

Excitement splashed over his face. He just knew he was getting it, but good, tonight. He approached puppy-dog smile and all. He puffed out his chest and winked at me like he was Tarzan or something. I turned my chin to my left shoulder with an inquisitive glance that he took as an invitation to drop his tattered shorts and pose. That about killed it for me; seeing him profiling like I was craving it or something.

Go Write and You Won't Go Wrong – How to Write Your Book in 30 Days!

So that's why I say, "Kill the critic." Sure, we'll resurrect this inner voice when the time is right. After all, an excellent critique can strengthen a good manuscript and make it great. Don't allow your judge to sentence your writing to life imprisonment. Keep the judge and critic out of your writing. Go for broke. Let it all spew out.

Books by Michael Ray King

Mel Johnson

Pets

The first family pet I remember was Lady, a gentle sweet miniature collie who followed me everywhere. Growing up as kids, my family always had pets.

Great with us kids, I don't ever remember Lady snipping at us even once, unlike Pugsy, the small Pekinese dog we had after Lady.

Two doors down from us, across the street, was Paul Walker's house. His daughter Judy was a year older than me and recently told me she remembered Lady grabbing my little brother by the diapers and tugging him home when my mom called us in for dinner. I don't remember that, but Lady was very smart so it's entirely possible.

Fetching a rubber ball was also one of her favorite games. When nobody was around to throw the ball so she could chase after it, Lady would chase cars.

As intelligent, gentle, and sweet as Lady was, she couldn't resist chasing cars. Our house was on the corner of Hammond and Westward Drive, so we had traffic passing in front, and on the east side, of our house. Lady would wait on the sidewalk for a car to pass by and then rush toward the street to chase it, yapping excitedly the entire length of our lot, 75 feet, three feet away from the passing vehicle. She wasn't growling in anger, it sounded more like fun.

Our attempts to discourage her from that potentially dangerous game were not successful. Her enjoyment chasing those cars was such that we could not dissuade her. Lady wouldn't chase them past our hundred-foot back lot line on the Hammond side, and would only chase those cars on the Westward side lot line-to-lot line 75 feet across the front. If they went east, down Westward Drive in front of our house the chase would stop when the asphalt of Hammond was reached. Cars turning south off of Westward Drive onto Hammond were fair game for the entire 100 feet our lot was deep. When the alley at the back of our lot was approached, Lady would reluctantly pull up hard, allowing the vehicle to escape.

Some of the people in the neighborhood complained about Lady chasing their vehicles but we didn't know how to stop her, short of locking her up all day. My dad grew up with hunting dogs in the country and the thought of tying her up for long periods all day was simply not acceptable to him.

Very protective of our family and perhaps Lady thought those cars were a threat to be run off. The only time I ever remember her growling low was at strangers who occasionally stopped by the house to visit or to buy lemonade from our little stand in front during the summer.

Or maybe she just loved running and chasing the cars. Or both.

In any case, one Saturday afternoon when I was nine or ten I saw her take off after a white Ford that was heading across the front yard on Westward, scrambling alongside the vehicle, yapping energetically. The speed limit on Westward Drive was thirty but few people heeded it. Slowing down as it approached Hammond, I was sure it was preparing to turn right.

Being on the right side of a vehicle turning right, onto Hammond, was a deadly combination. Before she could slam her paws into the turf or duck away, the right front wheel of the turning car hit her in the head and spun her around at least six times, like a spinning top, paws straight out to the side, tail and face flat. By the time the spinning stopped the white Ford was long gone. Us kids were horrified, crying out to each other, as she wasn't moving.

My mom, heard our cries, came quickly, immediately became hysterical, like the rest of us. Lying on the edge of the road, dried blood trickled from Lady's mouth. Over a ten-minute timeframe we edged closer, fearing the worst. Fortunately, the wheel had hit her a glancing blow and just knocked her unconscious. *That SOB in the car never even stopped to see how she was! He doesn't care! That's our dog!*

Then her head twitched a little, and gradually moved a little more. Eventually lifting her head up, Lady shook her head stronger, as if to rid herself of the cobwebs in her brain. "Look! Look! She's moving her head! Even raising it! Maybe she'll live after all! Hooray!"

Lady might endure that solid headshot but maybe her brain will be damaged. I'm afraid of losing her entirely or keeping only a part of her. She might not recognize us anymore, or want to play with us if her brain is injured.

Shaking her head a couple more times hard, Lady lifted her head up and sat up on her forelegs, looking around in a daze, her eyes glassy. A final last stronger headshake and her eyes began to focus. Hearing familiar voices in us kids and my mom, inching closer, her ears perked up and she stood up on all four wobbly legs.

" Look, she's standing! Yay! She can walk! Come her girl! Let me take a closer look at you." Cheers broke out among us as she shakily began wobbling toward us, her tail wagging, as usual.

Us kids began petting her and my mom scolded her gently. "Now let this be a lesson to you Lady. Don't you chase any more cars! We thought you were a goner!" Relief flooded through all of us.

Soaking up all the attention, affection, and thankful heartfelt petting for ten minutes Lady seemed to be back to normal and we returned to our usual activities playing in the front yard.

Fortunately or unfortunately, our dear family pet also returned to her normal activities too, which included chasing cars.

As sweet, gentle, and protective as Lady was, learning-from-experience was not her strong suit. Within a week passing cars were once again being actively pursued with great gusto.

Two months later, in the summer when it gets dark late, after a strong rainstorm, during dinner, everybody at our dinner table heard an ominous thump from in front of the house. We immediately knew something solid had been hit in the street in front of our house.

Fearing the worst, we all rushed to the large front window and once again saw Lady lying still at the edge of the road, three feet from where she had been hit before. "Oh no! She's been hit again!" we cried. "Let's wait and see if she'll get up again, like last time." my mom said, hoping.

Ten minutes later there was still no movement and my dad was volunteered to go check on her. Reaching her lifeless body he didn't touch her, just shook his head back and forth so we would know from the front picture window she wasn't going to be getting up. Returning to the house my dad pulled my mom to the side and I heard him whisper, "There's tire tracks right over her head and there's blood seeping from her ears. I'm going to get a shovel and bury her in the back yard.".

I was about ten years old and the eldest child. Lady had been my dog for most of my life so my dad let me see her before he lowered her into the eighteen-inch deep by ten inches wide hole he dug in the back yard, next to the alley. "I know you loved Lady, as we all did, but you are the oldest and mainly fed and took care of her so you can say goodbye to her if you want, before I bury her."

My chest tight and hurting, I could barely talk. All that came from my lips was a barely audible heartbroken "goodbye Lady." before collapsing into my dad's arms. He also found it hard to speak and it was the only time in my life I saw his eyes swell up. After five minutes he released me, telling me to go inside. "I want to get this finished before it gets dark. Go along now, son." picking up his shovel.

Lifting lady's body up carefully with the shovel he lowered it into the hole. I waited until her body wasn't visible anymore before returning to the house. My dad made a little wooden cross for her grave and I returned to it every day for about three weeks before school started. Homework, school and Life intervened and my visits became less and less frequent over time as my sadness abated.

A couple months later my mom adopted a Pekinese puppy from the Humane Society and named him Pugsy, for his pug face. A cute black and white mask, short tiny legs, and an entitled attitude were his outstanding characteristics. He became an "inside" dog, as opposed to Lady, who had spent most of her life in the doghouse my dad built in the back yard.

Prancing around the house like a bantam rooster, Pugsy acted like he owned the joint. My mom's youngest daughter no longer a baby, she adored and thoroughly spoiled Pugsy. Expensive "wet" food, a brush to comb him out, and a comfortable soft indoor sleeping pad were provided for him to lounge on.

Accustomed to special treatment, he didn't mind growling at you and even giving you a snip with his teeth if you displeased him. A couple toddlers were nipped when they patted his head hard instead of petting him gently.

Pugsy grew on you though, and after a while he was fully accepted as a valued member of the family. His Napoleonic attitude and strutting was cute, something to see, for a little two-pound fur ball.

Eight or nine years passed and Pugsy became old and even crankier than usual. My mom took him to the veterinarian who diagnosed him with old age and arthritis. His usual liveliness in movement and energy was lost. Moving around became slow and painful, so he basically stopped moving much. Food had to be carried to his throne and Pugsy required somebody to carry him outside to do "his business." Eventually losing control of his bladder and bowels, he required a doggy diaper. Cataracts on both of his eyes rendered him virtually blind.

The last straw for my mom was when we watched Pugsy whimpering in agony as he slept. The aching in his joints and bones couldn't be escaped or relieved, even in sleep.

I went with her for support when we took Pugsy to the vet for the last time. *I know this final decision is upsetting her.* Hugging him carefully in the lobby for the last time to avoid causing him any further pain her sweet words mingled with tears. "You have been my baby all your life and I've loved you like you were my child. (sob) I'll miss you terribly, Pugsy." Moisture streaked her cheeks, dripping off her chin without any obvious awareness or concern from her. A paper towel was offered and quickly became damp.

After five minutes of murmured goodbyes, sobs, sighs, and long tortured silences, seeing my mom was struggling to let go, the vet, Dr. Robertson, a kind and gentle guy in his forties who had cared for him from puppyhood, finally put his hands under Pugsy's sides and gently took possession of him.

"Let me have him, Missus J. It's time. He's old, hurting, and suffering. After all these years, I too, hate to watch him agonize and hurt. Our dear old friend needs relief."

Nodding at me to escort my mom out the door, I too struggled with the finality and irreversible consequences of our decision, choking up with sadness for her and Pugsy. "I don't want to leave him to die alone…yet I also don't want to watch him suffer either. I don't know what to do!" My mom was overwhelmed.

Eventually Dr. Robertson and his white coat disappeared thru the swinging door to the back room holding Pugsy very carefully and gently waist-high in front of him, and we reluctantly tore ourselves away, tearful, sad and mourning already.

Driving her home through the dark clouds and steady rain, we intellectually knew the right thing had been done. That discussion and cognitive knowledge didn't help the pain, sadness, or sense of familial loss in our hearts much.

I hurt as much for my mom and her suffering as Pugsy and his.

So, yes, I have known both the agony and the ecstasy of having pets.

About My Story

When I first took the PETS challenge, I didn't think there would be much for me to say, as I don't currently have a pet and haven't had one for the past ten years. This situation is sometimes due to landlord restrictions.

As I began thinking about it, fond memories returned about Lady and Pugsy. Memories I hadn't visited for years. Most of them were warm and pleasant thoughts and feelings. I realized while writing this that pets had been a big part of my life growing up. I miss that love and affection I shared with those animals. They brought a great deal of joy and fun to my life, two things which have been sadly missing lately. Once I buy my own place I plan to return to the Humane Society and rescue a pooch or two!

About the Author – Mel Johnson

Beau Johnson lived in a Miami suburb for over fifty years and worked in Mental Health throughout South Florida for over twenty of those years. Retiring in 2007 he moved to Palm Coast, Florida, deciding to become a writer in that same year. Liberating Rhonda is a coming-of-age tale set in the sixties in The Midwest. It's the first part of an Adult Fiction trilogy he is writing about, loosely based on an old girlfriend in Miami he knew during that time. The sixties were a time of Civil Right marches and demonstrations, Women's' Liberation, expanding boundaries and sexual mores and freedoms.

His first short story published is Bob ad Marie, an end-of-life love story about Alzheimer's Disease and its effects on caregivers. He writes in self-defense, to keep his brain active and sharp.

Excerpts from Mel's books

Liberating Rhonda

The 'Thank-you-for-being-there-for-me' kiss soon gained passion, tongue, and intensity as Rhonda started cupping Gwen's face in her hands and depositing light affectionate kisses all over. Strategic warm kisses rained softly down her neighbor's neck and shoulders, inciting serious groans of pleasure to escape her throat.

Liberated Rhonda

"I love to lie out in the sun, don't you, Mike?
He nodded.
"Well then, you and I have something else in common! We both love to sunbathe topless!" she smiled almost innocently. "Did you happen to drive by yesterday around two? I was catching some rays in the back yard." she nonchalantly asked, grinning.

Books by Mel Johnson

T.G. Agin

Test of Honor

Ike stretched, yawned, then relaxed to the sound of pounding surf and the gurgle of running water. *Running water!* Ike swung his legs out of the bunk as he blinked his eyes rapidly to clear them of sleep. His feet hit the floor with a splash. He stood naked, knee deep in water, and hit the light switch. Probably not the smartest thing to do, but he wasn't yet fully awake. The lights came on but flickered a bit. Ike waded toward the sound of water and flipped open the hatchway leading into the engine bay. He peered inside and detected turbulence in the black water on the port side of the hull.

Damn line must have come off a seacock. Ike inhaled several quick, deep breaths and ducked underwater. He stretched out his long, muscular arm, squeezed it between the port engine and the boat's hull, then worked his way aft. His fingers told him the story as he checked each connection and finally found the broken one. The hose floated free, and a steady gush of water flowed through the valve. Ike grabbed the handle and pulled, struggling due to the awkward angle, until it finally closed. The water slowed then stopped. Careful not to snag anything delicate on the engine as he went, Ike shimmied his way backwards to the hatch. The lights failed as he broke surface.

Ike climbed out of the engine bay and into the cockpit. The boat sat low in the water but did not appear in immediate danger of going under. That was the good news. The bad news was: no power, so the bilge pumps couldn't work. He'd need to get help.

Still nude, Ike stood on the aft deck of the boat in the early morning light, pondering his next move, when he heard, "Hey, neighbor. Looking good." Ike looked over and spotted a nicely groomed man wearing a housecoat and leisurely enjoying a morning cocktail on a boat three slips away. Ike flipped him the bird and went below.

Everything in the cabin floated or had sunk in the deep water except for the cell phone lying on top of Ike's dresser. He rummaged through the closet, pulled out a pair of shorts and a Hawaiian shirt, grabbed a pair of sandals, and went to the nightstand for his Colt 1911. Ike's hands, slick with grease from the engine room, fumbled the gun when he picked it up. His trusty weapon dropped behind the stand and disappeared into the inky water. He spent a couple unsuccessful minutes feeling for it with his feet before abandoning the search.

"Crap!" Ike's blood pressure rose a notch. He snatched open a drawer where he kept his backup handgun, but the only thing he could find in the dark turned out to be an old wrist-rocket sling shot. Of course, the pouch that held the metal-ball ammunition for it remained impossible to locate. A maniacal giggle started in the back of Ike's throat, but he suppressed it, added the slingshot to the stack of clothes, and moved out on deck where he could see. He wrung out his clothes as best he could then dressed under the appreciative gaze of his neighbor.

Ike walked the dock to the manager's office. Once there, he could make arrangements for a pump and contact his insurance company. The boat had undoubtedly suffered water damage, but if he worked quickly he could keep it to a minimum.

Crunch!

The noise caught Ike's attention. He looked for the source of the sound in the parking lot then went pale. An immense antique four-door Cadillac sat on his beloved Harley, which he had parked in its usual spot the day before. Ike cursed and ran the length of the dock, up the gangway, and through the parking lot, arriving at the scene as an ancient-looking lady extracted herself one arthritic limb at a time from the metal leviathan and shuffled to the rear of the gigantic car to see what she hit.

Ike resisted the urge to choke her to death as she apologized in a shaky voice, tears flowing, for bumping into his "little bike." She'd crushed the rear fender, broken the taillight, knocked the rear tire off its rim, and caused myriad paint scrapes as the falling bike hit the pavement. Ike stared at the mess lying before him. After a few long seconds he shook himself, pulled out his phone to take pictures, typed the woman's information into the phone's notepad, and called the police.

Bob, the marina manager, jogged over. "Oh, wow. Sorry, Ike. You get it sorted out?"

"Yeah, it's getting there, but this is the least of my worries. My boat's flooded. Do you have a pump?"

"No, but Sea-Tow does. They can be here in about ten minutes. I'll call them."

"Ahhh…I let my membership expire. This is going to cost me, but call them anyway. No choice."

"Okay, Ike." Bob punched numbers into his cell phone and arranged for the Sea-Tow guys to come straight over.

Satisfied that help was on the way, Ike went out to the boat and, after a few minutes of rummaging in the dark, found his wallet then returned to the scene of the collision. Flashing lights and the whoop of a police car's siren drew everyone's attention. The small crowd flocking around the sad scene backed out of the way as the cruiser rolled to a stop. The officer emerged from the vehicle and walked over with a clipboard in his hand. The tearful old lady and Ike took turns giving their information to the cop. The Sea-Tow guys arrived, and after several more minutes of paperwork and credit cards, Ike cleared them to get busy pumping out his boat. He finished the report with the officer and helped the old lady painstakingly insert herself back into the giant sedan. The officer, Ike, and several bystanders lifted her car's bumper off the motorcycle and watched as she drove, barely visible behind the steering wheel, out of the parking lot without further incident. The officer handed Ike a copy of the report and drove off. The bystanders dispersed and Ike lifted his bike back on its wheels, flipped the kickstand into place, and leaned it carefully on the rest. It stood solid on the kickstand, so he unclenched the bars and stepped away. Ike stood there for a minute, taking slow deep breaths, calming himself, when his phone rang.

"Hello."

"Hey, Ike. Steve, here. I've got a job for you, and it needs to be done fast."

"Not a good time, Steve."

"No, dude. You can't do this. We're best friends! Besides, you owe me, and I'm calling it in. I need you here at the store *now*!"

Ike shuddered, and his face took on a little color. "Okay. Let me figure something out. I'll be right there." Ike hung up, trying to determine how he was going to get over to Steve Warwick's place.

Bob had overheard part of the conversation. "You having mobility issues?"

"Yeah. Warwick needs me now. I have to find a ride."

"Got what you need sitting over there." Bob pointed behind him at the office.

The two men walked to the marina office. Sitting there in all its rusted Italian glory was an old Vespa Sprint 150.

"It looks like crap, but it runs. Bring it back in one piece. You break it, you buy it," Bob said.

Ike stared at the sad little machine. "How could you tell if I broke it?"

Ike retrieved his sunglasses from the broken Harley, stepped into the scooter, flipped the key, and kicked it to life. The quiet tat-tat-tat-tat of the two-stroke almost killed the deal, but Ike swallowed his pride, revved the throttle, and rode off. Steve had called in his favor and, despite the day's challenges, Ike was honor bound to do his best.

Buzzing along A1A, Ike wondered how much worse the day could get. A whole new definition of "when it rains, it pours" was in the works. He looked left at the ocean and contemplated going for a long swim when he saw a dolphin jump and wave at him. It seemed to say, "Suck it up, buddy; it's just life giving you a few lemons." A squadron of pelicans formed on the right and flew in formation with the Vespa as it rolled merrily south with its oversized cargo. Ike started to relax under the drone of the scooter, the warm sun, and his pleasant escort. The pelicans finally peeled off at the edge of Flagler Beach and rolled left out to sea. The last one dropped a nice deposit across the front of the Vespa and Ike.

"Jesus H. Christ! Can't a guy get a break?" Ike struggled to maintain control on the pelican-poop-slickened road. Bits of nastiness blew off the scooter's fairing and onto Ike's shirt and face. He wiped at his sunglasses, which smeared the mess around worse, and carefully kept his mouth shut. Thankfully, as he was riding nearly blind, Steve's shop was just a block ahead.

Ike parked out of sight behind the store and shut off the Vespa. Grabbing a handful of grass, he wiped at the pelican mess on his shirt. It blended with the pattern, but the processed-fish smell was something else. He walked inside.

"Whew! Oh my God. What stinks?" Steve fanned the air and tried not to choke. The customers in the store all pinched their noses, some of them gagging and making faces at Ike as they stampeded for the door.

"Don't ask. Do you have a rag or some paper towels? And what's the damn crisis?"

Steve had never experienced Ike's anger and quickly fetched some paper towels. He handed them over with a light shake in his hands.

"You kn- kn- know how I want to install a coffee bar here? Well, Becky called and told me somebody put a commercial espresso machine out on the curb with a 'Free' sign on it. It looks like it's in perfect condition. A machine like that is worth a couple thousand dollars." Steve shook his head. "Rich people. Anyway, I can't close the shop—too many customers. Becky had to leave, so she can't get it. I need you to run down there and pick it up before someone else does."

Ike stared at Warwick for a minute. "You're kidding. My boat almost sank, some ol' lady ran over my bike, I'm soaked in pelican crap, and you want me to go get a junk espresso machine. That's what you're calling in a favor for?"

Steve paused for a second, looking at Ike. "Gosh, I didn't realize you were having a rough morning." He scrunched his face apologetically and half shrugged. "But you're here now so might as well go get it. Right?" Steve smiled and held up his fist for a bump.

Ike pondered his friendship for a long minute, considered prison time, and decided something positive might as well come out of this mess.

"Got it, bro." His face blank, Ike turned, leaving Steve's fist hanging in the air, and walked out the door. Steve propped it open behind him to air out the store.

"If your bike is down, what are you driving?"

"Don't ask." Ike disappeared behind the shop. The Vespa started with a ring-ding-ding then settled into its steady, quiet tat-tat-tat. He crushed the grip in his huge paw, twisted the throttle, and buzzed away.

Ike mumbled and fumed to himself as he drove through town. He used the side streets to avoid being seen as best he could. It didn't work. A number of people he knew pointed at him and talked amongst themselves as he rode past. Rolling up on 18th Street, Ike spied a man studying the espresso machine. *Oh Hell no,* thought Ike. He stopped beside the man and said, "That machine's mine. I got over here as soon as I found out about it. Leave it alone. You follow?"

The man laughed. "Yeah, right. 'First come, first served' is the only rule on this stuff, and I'm taking it." The machine was big and heavy. He grabbed it with his arms, grunting as he lifted, and started towards a blue pickup truck.

Ike's face turned red. "I want that machine. Put it down *now*." He started to lose his cool a bit.

"Stuff it, buddy." The man continued towards the truck in short, staggering steps.

Ike thought of several options, none pretty, but they were a bit extreme for the situation. Suddenly he remembered he'd armed himself before leaving the boat. Reaching behind his back, he pulled the wrist rocket out of his pocket. Ike ran up behind the man, stretched the sling shot as far as he dared, released, and snapped it against the guy's ass where it joined his leg. The empty leather pocket of the slingshot struck with a stinging slap and bit deep into the soft skin. The man screamed and staggered around in circles, releasing his grip on the espresso machine so he could grab his butt. Ike quickly grabbed the machine before it could hit the ground. The injured man hopped and swore, holding his wounded ass with both hands.

Yeah, he's gonna have a massive bruise. Bet he won't cross me next time. Ike walked quickly to the Vespa, pushed along by the fountain of curses spouting from the injured man. He tucked the big coffee machine under one powerful arm then kicked the Vespa to life and wobbled along the street, trying to gain speed. The man cussed a blue streak, calling Ike every name in the book and adding a few new ones. Ike accelerated carefully and, a couple blocks later, built up enough speed so that no man alive could run and catch him. He started to smile until he remembered stopping could be an issue, as the espresso machine currently occupied his clutch hand.

Deal with that issue when it's time, he thought.

Ike rolled through stop signs and lights. His luck seemed to improve as no cops spotted him and, despite some near misses, he didn't get run over. When he swerved into Warwick's parking lot, he killed the engine and let the bike chug to a stop. Exhaling with relief, Ike dumped the scooter and went inside. With a grunt, he hefted the big machine onto the counter. "Here's your damn coffee machine. I'm out of here. Don't call me for a couple days. You follow?"

Steve looked sheepish while trying not to breathe through his nose. "Okay, buddy. Thanks. Let me know if you need any help with the boat. Oh wow! Check your arm. You're bleeding."

Ike looked at his left forearm. Blood trickled out of a gash he must have received from the coffee machine. It ran diagonally through the skull of his tattoo like a prohibition sign and would leave a nice scar. Ike didn't say a thing, turned, walked outside, lifted the fallen

Vespa with one hand, and stomped on its kick starter. He kicked it six times before he remembered to turn the key. As Ike pulled out of the gravel lot with the throttle twisted to its stop, he felt the rear tire spin and sling some stones. The corner of his mouth ticked up in a hint of a smile that didn't stay.

A couple miles from Steve's place, Ike approached The Iron Boot Saloon. He licked his lips then regretted it as he tasted pelican crap. *I really need a drink.* Ike pulled over and parked the scooter behind the building. The smell of stale beer and urine pretty much matched his pelican-enhanced shirt, so nobody noticed anything but Ike's size as he ducked through the doorway to enter the establishment.

"Give me a Bud. Make that two," Ike called to the bartender.

"You forget it's Sunday? New blue laws went into effect today. No alcohol sold or served until after midnight."

Ike stared. "You've got to be kidding me."

"Nope. I've got water, some soda, and milk. What'll you have?"

Ike muttered under his breath, "Soda."

The bartender rummaged in the fridge. "All I have left is ginger ale. That okay?"

"Sure. Whatever. I just need something to drink." Ike snatched the soda from the bartender, chugged a huge gulp, and coughed. The ginger fizz bubbled straight into his lungs, and he couldn't stop hacking.

Ol' Toothless, the wino, watched for a minute, grinned, and cackled. "Too strong fer ya? Here, let me buy you some milk." He plunked a dollar on the bar and started belly laughing. The rest of the Boot's patrons joined in until the sound became overwhelming.

Ike continued to cough, tears rolling down his cheeks. He closed his eyes as he choked and then felt lightheaded. When he opened them, the room swirled and he fell into darkness.

Eventually, Ike woke. The floor felt way too soft and cushy. A cloth lay over him, and the room gently rocked.

"What the Hell?" He looked around as his head cleared and realized he was in bed, under the covers, on his boat. Puzzled, he turned on the lights and looked around. Dry as a bone. No gurgle of water; only the pounding of surf. Getting out of bed, he walked to the cockpit and looked at the parking lot. The Harley sat there peacefully, undamaged, just as he'd left it the night before.

"Looking good, neighbor." The voice came from a gentleman three boats from his who saluted Ike with a cocktail-laden hand.

Ike realized he stood nude on the deck, flipped the guy the bird, and then went below. Ike shook his head, grabbed the big flat box off the kitchen counter, went back out on deck, and pitched the box's contents over the side. He swore never again to eat sushi, shrimp, and anchovy pizza before bed.

Precious Cargo

The little schooner died that night. Rock talons tore open her belly. Broaching as waves filled her hold, she found her grave in the shallows. Escaping mostly unharmed, the small crew made their way to the desolate beach. The helmsman received a well-deserved and thorough tongue lashing from the captain while the other men, turning to their survival, rounded up wood and quickly made a fire. Nothing further was to be done until sunrise, so the first watch was set and the rest slept.

Morning rose and saw the small vessel, beyond repair, firmly aground on her side. The men waded out to salvage what they could. Throughout the day weapons, food, and crates were collected then rope and sails cut loose to build a shelter.

The crew examined their hoard and secured the gleanings near their camp. The day wore on; tropical heat sapped their strength. At dusk the last chest— large and old with a padlocked hasp—was ready for examination. With hammer and chisel they broke the lock and pried open the lid.

The men peered into the chest, started then stood open mouthed. A beautiful red-haired young woman lay curled on her side as if asleep. Thick tufted, green velvet cushions surrounded and cradled her. Aromatic herbs and dried flowers lay thickly about her body to mask the ancient, musty air.

"Mother of God! There's a dead woman in there. Why the Hell wasn't that marked?" The captain crossed himself as he stepped away from the chest. "It's too late now to deal with properly. Close the lid and we'll bury her in the morning."

Mike the helmsman, armed with sword and musket, stood first watch that evening. The wind in the trees set fronds and leaves shuddering. He thought he saw something move in the undergrowth then felt a gentle caress on his neck.

At dawn the fire was stoked and breakfast started. The captain studied his crew as they ate. "Mike? You feelin' okay? Your color's off."

"Not well, sir. I think I caught the fever last night during watch. Chill's been working me pretty hard."

Mike saw a bug scuttling through the sand. Grinning, he snatched it up and stuck it in his mouth. The captain shook his head and looked away.

The crew trudged out to perform the burial. Settling on a nice spot for the grave the crew proceeded to dig. They carried the chest to the hole, gently laid it in, and covered it. The captain said a prayer, crossed himself, and all returned to camp.

Over the following weeks the whole crew, one by one, caught the fever but recovered and continued the work of survival. Finally, a sail appeared. Lighting the signal fire, the boson waived his arms and screamed at the top of his lungs. The ship changed heading and sent a boat ashore.

The crew waited patiently, worshipful, surrounding the ancient chest. At last they would see their new mistress safely home.

About the Author – T. G. Agin

Timothy Agin is an aspiring writer working on his craft. He had over 10 years' experience as a technical writer for the Department of Defense before turning his hand to creating fiction. Tim's interest is primarily in science fiction where he has created a fantastic world of nanotechnology and genetic engineering. Beyond that realm, Tim also puts together short stories on random thoughts that skitter across his mind's eye.

In this anthology are two selections. The first, Precious Cargo, was created for a flash fiction contest and the second, Test of Honor, was for an anthology about another writer's character Ike.

Tim found Precious Cargo to be a great writing exercise. The 500 word limit for the composition forces the writer to pick each word carefully to extract the most impact.

Test of Honor was a fun romp with his friend, Tim Baker's, Ike character. The Ike stories follow the hero through multiple adventures in the local community. Tim Agin chose to give Ike a different kind of challenge than he usually deals with.

Tim, writing as T.G. Agin, is currently working on several novels and an anthology about his science fiction world of the Nanogen.